THE KINDLER

A TynkerVille Story

MICHAEL SOLIMANO

ISBN: 9798883062673

To my family, and those who work until
they hold their dreams in their hands.

Prologue

Kala Blaise stepped through TynkerVille's massive, rose gold doors for the very first time. She didn't notice the waterfall of molten silver flowing just yards away. Nor did the golden ivy, hand-twisted and climbing the inner walls of TynkerVille, catch her gaze.

Kala only saw the trees.

They had no bark, leaves or sap of any kind. They were sculpted from pure silver, from their branches right down to their roots. And there were hundreds of them; they made a metallic forest that stretched endlessly into the horizon.

"And you kept this all a secret?"

Bartie Flay's voice trembled with disbelief. The elderly man stood aghast beside Kala, watching the silver trees. Both had

1

won a tour of the reclusive TynkerVille factory. They were the first outsiders to lay eyes on the inside of the metal building.

"All this silver... and you never thought to share?"

All the locals, Bartie included, always thought a simple toy factory hummed inside the walls of TynkerVille. Where else could all of the Tynks—those gorgeous, steel toys—be coming from? Instead there was this silver forest, hidden away from all of them.

"Today's schedule has changed," announced a voice. It spoke from everywhere at once, as if the air of TynkerVille was talking. "*The Day with the Designer...* your so-called *Tour of TynkerVille...* is no more."

"Lies!" Bartie cried, whipping his cane through the air.

"Today's prize is too precious to be given away," the voice continued. "TynkerVille's prize must be earned."

With a resounding crack, TynkerVille's massive entry doors slammed shut. Outside, the city of Holloton and its huge crowds vanished. The sole exit from TynkerVille was sealed.

"We were promised a day with the Designer!" Bartie roared. "All your pamphlets... they said we'd each get one-of-a-kind Tynks!"

Bartie was the lone voice cutting into the silence. Kala Blaise and two other tour winners remained mute, their eyes fixed on TynkerVille's sealed doorway.

"Deals change," TynkerVille's voice went on. "We've decided to add a little *spice* into the mix. That's why you're all here — to watch how TynkerVille makes beautiful things from chaos!"

The voice converged into a single point: it was the Designer speaking, the reclusive owner of TynkerVille. He was perched on a silver branch, juggling three huge gemstones. An emerald, a ruby, and a black diamond, each the size of a closed fist.

Tossing aside these priceless gems, the Designer unveiled his real treasure: a platinum Tynk fully studded with diamonds. The metal toy gave off a ghostly green mist as its outer rings turned around an inner sphere.

"Look at it!" the Designer shouted, tossing the Tynk high into the air. It arced over his silver forest, hovered for a moment, then started falling. As this happened, TynkerVille's silver forest came alive. Its branches began twisting and turning. They caught the falling Tynk and whisked it out of sight.

"Welcome to *The TynkerVille Trial!*" the Designer cackled. His eyes shimmered with mischief. "Here's how it works. Find my Tynk and you'll be crowned winner. Fail, and you'll be sent somewhere less *shiny.*"

A shiver ran through Kala. In an instant, her tour of TynkerVille had morphed into something very different.

She watched the Designer leap from his silver tree, land silently on TynkerVille's marble floor, and start yanking on a silver tree root. It was a lever that opened a gaping hole in the floor as it pumped up and down. A hideous smell rose from this pit: filth and disease wound together.

"Let's be perfectly clear," the Designer said, pinching his

nose. "Find my Tynk… or rot in my sewers!"

***

No, we're getting ahead of ourselves. Tynks, the Designer, metal castles, rotten sewers… they don't mean anything to you.

Not yet.

If you want to understand any of this, we have to go back. We have to travel somewhere less grand. Into the basement of an ancient library… that's where our story begins.

<u>1</u>

But this is no ordinary library. And where we're headed is no ordinary night.

Imagination itself hangs by a thread, and one family's tapestry is about to unravel.

A Dusty Closet in the Basement of The Holloton Library
December 14th, 1197 | 11:28pm

"Is your mother asleep?" Mortimer Blaise whispered. "Did she put out her fires?"

"I don't care if she hears us," Kala Blaise answered.

"She has to be asleep if we're going to do this."

"I saw her walk upstairs, okay? Her fires are out, too," Kala huffed. "She made we read two whole books today. Two! Can you believe her?"

Mortimer grinned. "A true Kindler is lost in literature from dawn until dusk," he quipped, playfully mimicking his wife. "They dream in stories and wake in poetry."

Kala sighed. "I hate when she says that."

"Don't we all?"

Mortimer and Kala met each other's eyes and smiled. They huddled over a watchmaker's table that was littered with old, metal gears.

They were not supposed to be here.

Kala's mother, Luana Blaise, had strictly forbidden it. She said Kala's time was best spent reading and writing, not building "useless tinkerings" in a broom closet. Yet here they were, father and daughter, tucked away in their underground watchmaking club.

Mortimer leaned in, a secret perched on his lips. "That moonwatch we made is nothing compared to my new idea," he whispered, revealing a crumpled sketch. "Look at it… a clock that runs backwards!"

He uncrumpled his drawing for Kala and his smile danced with mischief. But then, Mortimer stopped. There was a creak in the ceiling… was Luana still awake?

"Don't be so afraid of her," Kala said. "She'd never hurt you."

"You don't know her power," Mortimer breathed, his eyes still tethered to the ceiling. "Being Kindler doesn't mean she has control over it."

Kala rolled her eyes and seized her father's drawing. "A backwards clock? Who would ever want one of those?"

"No one's bought any of my watches in years," Mortimer sighed. "But this… this would never be for sale. It's much too powerful."

"How?" Kala asked.

"You don't know its secret." Mortimer curled a bushy eyebrow. "If we follow this drawing exactly—and I mean not a single screw out of place—this clock will perform magic… it will take us back in time!"

Kala snorted as another crack rang from the ceiling. This time, Mortimer's hand was swift to silence her. Footsteps, like the ticking of a clock, began pacing overhead.

In a flurry of motion, Mortimer stowed his watch gears out of sight. "Hide yourself," he said. "Pretend you're sleeping in the roots. The clock can wait!"

Kala nodded silently. She shuffled over to the closet's door, but hesitated before leaving. "Tomorrow night we're building that clock," she whispered. "Mom can't always get her way."

But Mortimer hardly heard her. His attention was fixed on the footsteps upstairs. His chest quivered and his eyes started glistening in the room's dim candlelight.

Was Mortimer crying? Or was he just tired?

Kala couldn't tell. She knew her father looked tiny inside this makeshift workshop. The objects stacked around him—barrels of stale ink, moldy reams of paper, towers of old books—seemed huge in comparison.

It was then Kala realized how little her father truly owned. There was his broken watchmaker's table and a bag full of rusted gears, but nothing more. Everything else in the Holloton Library belonged to Kala's mother.

"It won't always be like this," Kala breathed.

She turned away, leapt up the basement's staircase and came upon a sight that never failed to steal her breath away. It was the library's Gathering Room, a cathedral of stories whose walls were lined with book spines and winding ivy. The air in the room was thick with whispers of old stories. At its center stood an ancient yew tree, old as mountains and fat as a house.

The yew tree cradled twenty-three books on its limbs, each of them written by Kala's ancestors, the Kindlers. But the yew tree's true jewel lived on its highest branch. There, a blue fire named Aeverum simmered. It was the source of all the world's Imagination. For centuries, it had been replenished when Kindlers told stories in the Holloton Library.

Aeverum was usually a beacon of blue light, but tonight Kala struggled to see the fire. It had shrunk over the last year, shriveling down to the size of a closed fist.

Crack!

A branch snapped away from the yew tree and shattered against the floor. This happened often. The tree was centuries old, after all.

Ploosh!

But then, an old book fell from somewhere above. It

tumbled down and came to rest between two roots. Squinting, Kala read the letters that were etched into the book's binding.

The Far Reacher, by Quintessa Blaise.

Old branches might have fallen from time to time, but *this* simply didn't happen. The book on the ground wasn't some old folktale. It was a Kindler story, one of just twenty-three in the world.

Kala tucked herself between two of the yew tree's larger roots and looked for the source of the disturbance. She found the library totally silent, save for a lone figure. He cut through shadow and rounded the back of the yew tree.

Then, he climbed.

2

Kala Blaise was still as the night. Her eyes were locked on the stranger climbing her family's sacred yew tree.

He can't see me in the dark, Kala hoped.

Above, the stranger moved with scary strength. He ripped off huge pieces of bark and made the yew tree shake beneath his feet. More Kindler books fell from their branches and crashed in plumes of dust as they hit the ground.

What are you? Kala wanted to ask. She had never seen power like this.

The moon shone down and revealed the stranger's secret: his arms and legs were woven full of metal wires. His face was hidden behind a grey mask dotted with tiny, sparkling stones.

As he climbed, the metal wires cut into the stranger's skin

but failed to slow him down. He reached the top of the yew tree, where the blue fire Aeverum was still flickering. Then, he pulled a curious stone from his pocket that glowed with a soft, green light.

"You have to be patient," the stranger said, holding his stone up to Aeverum. "Give me time."

It was unclear who the stranger was speaking to. He waited a moment, holding out his stone, but nothing happened. Aeverum kept burning. The stone kept glowing.

"Take the fire!" the stranger hissed. He pushed the stone closer, but Aeverum twisted away and avoided his touch. "You didn't say the fire could move! I'll… I'll figure something out. Give me time!"

But a static noise filled the library. It was followed by the sound of ripping flesh. The barbs in the stranger's skin started twisting and curling. They shredded his skin and sent blood pumping from his wounds.

Kala watched, frozen, as the stranger fought the pain, tears trickling out from behind his mask. The awful noise stopped as quickly as it started, and the stranger collapsed, sobbing softly.

"I can take your pain," he breathed after a long spell.

He wiped away his tears, stood tall, and with a shout, he slammed his glowing stone down onto Aeverum. The branch holding the blue fire split in two. The first piece was left dangling from the yew tree. The second piece tumbled towards the floor. It landed beside a stack of old books and instantly set their bindings ablaze.

Whoosh! Blue flames leapt from bookshelf to bookshelf, and soon, the library's walls were a towering inferno.

But even as this happened, Kala didn't budge from her hiding spot. She kept her eyes on the stranger above. His demeanor changed as he watched his fires grow.

"No, I didn't want this," he said, his voice lost in the crackling fires. "This was *you*... you made me do this!"

3

Blue flames towered inside the Holloton Library. Smoke gathered beneath its ceiling, twisting and darkening the glass. Jars of ink couldn't withstand the heat, bursting with little pops and pings that punctuated the chaos.

Kala Blaise remained hidden in a maze of tree roots, a sanctuary from the licking flames and swirling smoke. High above, the metal stranger wasn't faring as well. He was losing his battle to a dark, thickening haze.

Overwhelmed, he sobbed amidst the roar of the fires and ran for the end of the yew tree. He leapt and fell in a silver streak, crashing near Kala with a force that splintered the yew's mighty roots.

The stranger lay gasping and groaning but was not injured.

His metal wiring protected him from that. The yew tree bore the brunt of his fall; a section of its ancient roots shattered into many pieces.

Watching this all, Kala's thoughts raced with memories of the library's darkest stories, the ones that spoke of creatures who could walk through fire without being burned.

Was that what this stranger was… a monster?

Kala shrunk further into her hiding place in the roots. She could hear the stranger whispering now, his murmurs blending with the crackling flames. He was arguing, but still, Kala didn't know with who.

Grumbling and groaning, the stranger stumbled towards the library's exit. But his footsteps suddenly veered sideward as he turned down the staircase that led into the library's basement where Mortimer Blaise was still tucked away.

"Dad, watch out!" Kala yelled. The words poured out before she could stop herself.

She thought of her father, slumped helplessly over his broken watch gears. What did Mortimer have to fight back with, a screwdriver?

Boom!

Wood snapped and crumbled somewhere up ahead. Kala feared for her father, but when she climbed out from the roots, she didn't see Mortimer or the metal stranger. The sound hadn't come from the basement. It was the library's massive entrance doors; they had just been kicked open.

A woman stood in the shattered doorway, her black hair

glistening in moonlight. Her blue eyes screamed with color, the very same sapphire as the library's fires.

This was Luana Blaise. Kala's mother. The Kindler.

Kala opened her mouth, a torrent of questions on her lips, but swallowed them. Now was not the time. Her father was in danger.

Kala dashed through the burning library, dodging falling books and leaping over scattered embers. She turned towards the basement but was cut short as her mother clamped a hand down on her shoulder.

"Save the Kindler books first, we can't replace them!" Luana gasped, looking out over the fiery ruins.

"But Dad…" Kala started.

Her mother smacked the rest of the words out of her mouth. "The library comes first," Luana seethed. "We have to take care of the fire. We're the only ones who can stop it!"

Kala's cheek stung and her eyes welled with tears. She couldn't understand her mother at all. A library could be rebuilt; a father was irreplaceable.

Luana charged into the inferno and waved for Kala to follow. "The fire will listen to you," she said. "You're a Kindler, Kala!"

But Kala hesitated as a familiar doubt crept into her bones. Was she really a Kindler? She wanted to believe her mother, but didn't know if she could.

For generations, women in the Blaise family had told stories in the Holloton Library to replenish Aeverum, the blue flame that lived atop the yew tree. It was the source of all the world's Imagination. So long as that flame burned, so did the minds of all living things.

Kala was next in line to be Kindler, and because she had no siblings, was the *only* one in line. But Kala hated reading stories and hated telling them even more. She'd never built a blue flame of her own, not even a wisp. She often wondered if she was adopted. Surely, she could not be Luana Blaise's daughter.

Yet you have the same hair as her, a clear voice swirled through Kala's mind. *And the same exact eyes. That's no coincidence.*

Kala didn't know what to think. She watched fires burn everywhere in the library, except along the yew tree. Its bark repelled the flames, protecting the few books still stacked on its limbs.

Luana was chasing after the rest of the Kindler books, the ones that had been kicked to the ground by the metal stranger. Many of these stories had already burned, but there were some left to be saved. Luana plucked them off the ground, patted down their fires and heaved them back onto the yew tree. It was the only safe place left in the library.

But soon, the fires around Luana grew too large for her to ignore. She paused her search and started weaving her hands through the air. Her long fingers flashed and twirled, and moments later, fire began bending to their will.

Luana twisted clouds of fire into hot spirals that vanished once they turned fast enough. She leapt through the library, weaving and twisting, but struggled to keep up with the growing flames.

"Don't watch," Luana screamed. "Help me, Kala!"

But Kala had still not moved from the front of the library. She looked into her palms and wondered what they were capable of. Did they also have ancient power? Could they also weave fire and make it vanish?

You're a Kindler, the clear voice in Kala's mind said. *The fire will listen to you.*

Kala felt something change in her chest. Hidden power stirred through her core and streamed to her fingertips. She ran over to a burning book and began weaving her fingers, just like her mother. Kala would wield this fire. She would be a Kindler.

But many seconds passed, and Kala's wriggling hands failed to move the flame. It kept on raging. It kept destroying the old book.

"Mom said I'm a Kindler," Kala snarled. "That means you listen to me!"

This time, Kala threw her hand on top of the burning book and snapped it shut. The blue fire quickly shriveled and died inside her fist.

Finally, a smile lit Kala's lips. "I did it... Mom, I can't believe I did it - *ah!*"

Only the fire hadn't listened to Kala at all. It hadn't shriveled or died, and instead, leapt around her closed fingers and scorched her. Kala screamed and fell to her knees as the skin of her hand turned bright red. Through tears, she watched her mother weave more fire near the base of the yew tree. The flames never touched Luana, always bending a safe distance around her.

You were wrong, Kala thought of her mother, gritting her teeth in pain. *I'm not like you. I'm not a Kindler.*

There was another crash at the front of the library as two figures came running up from the basement. The first was Mortimer Blaise. He bled from his forehead and clutched his bruised ribs. He was leading the second figure, the metal stranger, towards the library's shattered doors. Mortimer waved a tiny pair of golden scissors as he ran. It was the only thing he had to fight back with.

"Come on, a Kindler can't find what you need," Mortimer wheezed at the stranger. "A mind. That's what you really want... a mind like *mine!*"

Mortimer looked wild as ever. His hair was tossed in a grey tangle and his eyes were full of bulging veins. Even still, he struggled to hold the metal stranger's attention. His gaze had drifted back over the library, onto the inferno he made. He watched wood beams splinter and snap. He saw entire bookcases crumble into ash. More tears pooled beneath his silver mask.

Bzzz...

A familiar static filled the air as the metal stranger doubled over in pain once more. His metal barbs twisted and turned through his arms and legs.

"Stop it," he squealed. "Enough!"

Spit and blood dribbled through the stranger's mask. The

static noise died down, and when his torture was through, the stranger took four long breaths. He rose from his knees, turned towards Mortimer Blaise, and sprinted for him. The pair vanished out the library's crumbled doors and were lost to the night.

Kala was left alone in the heart of the inferno. She had a choice to make. She could chase after her father or run into the flames to help her mother.

Kala brought a hand to her swollen cheek. She let her thoughts drift to building watches in the basement. Her answer came easily.

"I'm sorry, Mom," Kala whispered.

The words hardly passed Kala's lips, but somehow, they carried all the way into her mother's ears. Luana Blaise was shattered when she heard them. She lowered her hands and let a cloud of flame consume her.

But Kala didn't see this. She was already sprinting into the night, leaving behind the fiery tomb of stories, chasing the fading echoes of her father and the metal stranger.

4

Outside, the night sky was ablaze. Snowflakes twinkled in the eerie blue light that came from the fire devouring the Holloton Library. Kala's breath misted in the freezing air as she ran, the ground hard and cold beneath her feet. Explosions from the library boomed like thunder, urging her forward as she tracked a path of bloody footprints that had been left in the snow by the metal stranger and her father.

Looking ahead, Kala searched for any sign of Mortimer. But all she saw were vultures circling the smoky sky and the dark, silent forest that bordered Holloton. Her neighbors, the Gallaghers, Shakes, and Grays, peered out from their homes, their faces bathed in blue light.

"My mom's still in there!" Kala screamed. "I... I couldn't

help her!"

But her neighbors were unmoved. Their expressions were etched with the stark realization that Kala had yet to accept: The Holloton Library was already lost.

"Do something!" Kala screamed.

But one by one, her neighbor's windows darkened as they snuffed out their candles. They disappeared from view, surrendering the library to its flames.

"Don't touch me!"

Kala's ears caught the distant sound of her father's voice, tinged with panic, and she sprinted forward. She followed the path of bloody snow out of Holloton and into the wilderness that surrounded the city.

In the forest's grip, Kala wove through rows of slender trees until she found a faint emerald glow. It came from a familiar, pock-marked stone and illuminated a violent fight. Mortimer and the metal man were wrestling on the forest floor.

"Stop fighting back!" the stranger hissed.

He struck Mortimer with a terrible crunch and sent him crumpling into the snow. Then, he seized a fistful of Mortimer's hair and drew his eyes upward until they were level with his pock-marked stone.

Kala's breath caught in her throat as she watched a smoky haze seep out from her father's eyes. It disappeared into the stone and vanished.

"Don't blink before the stone's done," the stranger warned Mortimer. "Or I'll cut your throat."

Desperate, Kala snatched a fallen branch from the ground and flung it with all the force she could muster. It struck the stranger's mask with a dull thud but failed to move him.

"What are you doing to him?" Kala screamed.

The stranger kicked the branch aside. His attention never wavered from his stone and Mortimer's fading eyes. "It's almost your turn," he called out to Kala, invitation in his voice.

Kala chucked another branch but missed the stranger terribly. "Stop it!" she sputtered.

"But we're just getting started," the stranger answered. "You have so much to learn, Kala Blaise."

"How... how do you know my name?" Kala whimpered.

Smoke continued to seep from Mortimer, and his life seemed to ebb away with each wisp that the pock-marked stone consumed. His body went limp, and Kala knew that whatever was being taken from him was precious and irreplaceable.

"I'm saving your father," the stranger said, tapping Mortimer's empty skull. "Saving him from his mind."

Kala tried to turn and run. But her body betrayed her and she remained stuck in place. Her gaze was locked on the pock-marked stone. She felt it pulling her forward. She watched a blue mist drift from her own eyes.

Kala heard the metal stranger's approaching steps as her vision started to speckle. More mist left her eyes, and the world became a blur. Her father's colorless pupils were the final image burned in Kala's mind before darkness consumed her.

<u>5</u>

August 15th, 1198 | 5:30pm
The Remains of the Holloton Library

I have to find it. I have to keep... digging!

Kala Blaise ripped open her hand. She used a melted watch gear, one of the few items that survived the library's fire. Its sharp edge bit into her skin, but she pushed through the sting.

Deeper, Kala thought. *Don't stop.*

Her hand opened up into a painful bloom of red. It should have made her flinch or cry out, but Kala remained focused. She was looking for something: a flash in her blood that she hoped would shimmer with blue, the same color as Aeverum's flame.

Above Kala, a broken yew tree stood watch. "I'm supposed to be Kindler," Kala whispered to the tree. "Can you help me find my fire?"

But the yew tree, and the few books left on its crooked limbs, stayed silent. They offered no help to the bleeding girl below.

"You talk to Mom," Kala said, her voice tinged with resentment. "Why won't you talk to me?"

Only the wind responded, a howl that carried the scent of char through the holes in the library's roof.

Kala's voice dropped to a hush. "You must think I'm a traitor," she said. "I can't remember why I ran from the library that night, but I promise, it wasn't to abandon you."

But still, the ancient books kept quiet. And Kala's palm kept bleeding.

***

On the other side of the yew tree, Luana Blaise read from a tattered book. Her face was marked with purple burn marks from the night of the fire. She was ashamed of them.

Just don't look up from the book, Luana told herself. *Oh, they're only children. Why do you even care? Get on with the story.*

Luana told a simple tale of two children who stumbled into a lion's den and tried to fight their way free. It wasn't a happy story. Luana didn't read those anymore.

"The boy dropped to the bottom of the pot as the lion paced around his sister. Lifting a single claw, the lion said—*Colin O'Claire, put that damn Tynk away!*"

The tale broke off.

Kala rounded the tree and found her mother. *You gave her those scars,* she thought bitterly. Avoiding her mother's face, she looked to the bookshelves around her. The once grand Holloton Library was now a graveyard of stories.

A memory haunted the edges of Kala's thoughts: a vision of a Kindler ensnared in a ring of fire. Kala reached out, desperate to save her mother, but her hands grasped only smoke as screams echoed around her.

Kala's memories of that night were a jigsaw with too many missing pieces. Only fragments of heat, fear, and the terrible sound of her mother's anguish remained.

"Colin, enough with that toy," Luana said.

Her voice was a sharp command that fell on the distracted ears of her tiny crowd. There was an old man with a patchy beard and whiskey on his breath sitting fast asleep. A few seats down were the Duckworth twins, Melissa and Gwen. They kicked each other in the shins, and when they got tired of fighting, they flicked ropes of snot onto the chairs in front of them. Last in the crowd was Colin O'Claire, the boy who sat staring into his shimmering palms. There, a steel disc spun around a copper orb. It was a gadget that looked something like a tiny, metal planet. It was called a Tynk.

These were the toys being sold by the TynkerVille Factory, each of them handmade by the Designer. He was the man who could bend any metal into any shape... the man who built a castle with a single pour of molten steel... the man with a golden monocle and a ruby eye...

Or so everyone said.

Everyone in Holloton had one of his Tynks. Well, *almost* everyone. Kala watched the Tynk spin, and a sense of déjà vu enveloped her. There was something about the green light it emitted, something achingly familiar. But she couldn't remember what.

"Colin, put that away or I'll turn it to dust," Luana warned again, a hint of strain in her voice.

She tapped against the yew tree and a charred book fell from somewhere above. It hit Colin right on the head and knocked his Tynk from his hands. The toy was sent rolling along the ground, and immediately, three small bodies dove on top of it.

It was Colin and the Duckworth twins, all wrestling for the fallen Tynk. They scratched, clawed, and shrieked aloud.

"It's mine!"

"I want it!"

"I *need* it!"

"ENOOUUGHH!!!!"

Luana Blaise had the last word. Something changed in her voice. It burst through the library like a bomb of wind, knocking the children flat on their backs. As she spoke, Luana took hold of a slender tree root. The yew tree above her started humming with blue light. At its top, Aeverum rippled and flared. For a moment, the yew tree, Luana and her blue fire were one. But the moment quickly passed.

Luana's fingers slipped off the root and her power vanished. Her hands fell to her knees and she hacked a wet cough into her sleeve.

"Those aren't just toys," she rasped, catching herself on her cane. "They'll destroy your minds if you let them."

No one answered. And with a long sigh, Luana disappeared around the yew tree.

"Is it your stomach again?" Kala asked, following her mother. "Ginger worked last time. I can find you some."

"It's Aeverum and you know it Kala. When the fire shrinks, I shrink with it. What's ginger going to do?" Luana let out another sigh. "You know, if Colin O'Claire's feet caught on fire, I doubt he'd even notice. As long as that *thing* keeps spinning."

"You mean the Tynk?"

"Don't say its name," Luana quipped. "Read for me tonight, Kala. We need a new Kindler. The children... they don't listen to me anymore."

"I can't. Not yet," Kala answered, her voice barely above a whisper.

"You can't keep running from who you are," Luana said. "You're the next Kindler. Aeverum needs you, Kala."

Kala's protest was cut short. Her mother lifted her hand and a weak tendril of fire emerged from her palm. It fell onto a thick root and raced up the yew tree to meet Aeverum. The blue flame flickered for a moment, then grew ever so slightly larger.

This was why Luana kept reading stories in her burnt library. It's why Aeverum was so much more than a simple, blue flame. There was far more at stake than books and storytelling.

There was Imagination itself.

But Luana's job had never been this difficult. No one listened to her stories anymore. They only cared about the metal toys, the Tynks, being sold by TynkerVille. Aeverum was dwindling, and so was the life of its Kindler.

"I'm empty, Mom. I can't find my fire," Kala said.

"You're not empty," Luana insisted. "You just haven't found your spark yet. Come sit with me." Luana's voice softened. "You owe it to yourself. To all of us."

Kala followed her mother back around the yew tree and onto a small reading stage.

"Alright, one more story tonight," Luana said, lifting *Holloton's Finest Short Stories: 1803* onto her lap. "How about Lost in The Clouds? Does that one work for you, Gwen?"

The library's tiny crowd was, surprisingly, still in their seats. Gwen Duckworth let out a *humph* in response to Luana's question, then kicked her sister in the shin.

"*Little runt,*" Luana muttered, then composed herself. "This is an old story. Just give it a chance, okay? It's about Gramblers, you may have heard of them."

Luana's next tale was even stranger than her first and Kala started to wonder if all the library's good stories were burned in the fire. It was a tale about creatures made of fog who stole a young girl from an ancient garden.

Luana read for a minute or so, then placed a hand on her stomach and shifted in her seat. She still looked weak and sickly.

"…*the Gramblers plucked poor Winnie right out from her garden.
They ripped her into the sky and locked her in the darkest cloud they
could find…*"

Beads of sweat started trickling down Luana's cheek. Her
hands shook.

"…*the Gramblers called Lightning and Thunder to keep Winnie
locked away. They called on h-hurricanes, and…*"

Luana struggled to keep her eyes open. Her words turned
to slurs. She coughed and specks of blood flew from her
mouth. The crowd hardly noticed the change in her story. The
Duckworth girls flicked each other's ears and Colin O'Claire
stared back into his Tynk.

The only one paying any sort of attention was the bearded,
old man. Awake, he looked at Luana and smiled. Then he
looked up to Aeverum.

What do you want with our fire? Kala wondered.

She followed the stranger's eyes to the top of the library and
gasped. A giant hole was wriggling in the middle of Aeverum
that made Luana shudder with each of its twists and turns.

The library's ancient fire, and its Kindler, were under attack.
Kala was sure of it.

"*Winnie Whittleworth…*" Luana heaved. "…*fought the…*"

"Quit reading!" Kala screamed.

She watched the old stranger wriggle his fingers inside his
coat.

"Are you moving the fire?" Kala shouted at him. "Stop it,

29

you're hurting her!"

The stranger slowly lifted his hand. Something glimmered inside his coat and jolted a memory onto Kala's eyes. She saw a flicker of the past... a man with metal wires laced through his limbs. She watched him strike Aeverum and set the Holloton Library ablaze.

"You were... you were there," Kala said. "The night of the fire... you started it!"

The stranger's fist kept rising from his coat. He was holding a tiny blade and pointing it right at Luana.

"Mom, he's back!" Kala shouted. "Run! Get behind the tree!"

The stranger rose from his chair as Luana coughed up more blood. He moved for the stage with mad, twinkling eyes.

Kala started to shout but went quiet as her fingers curled around something sharp in her pocket. It was her father's melted watch gear, the same one that sliced through her palm just minutes ago.

"Don't come any closer," Kala seethed.

"Leave him," Luana gasped beside her. "He's not... hurting me."

Kala wasn't listening to her mother anymore. She gripped the watch gear between her fingers and turned out its melted tip. She studied the stranger's green eyes and the way their veins popped and pulsed.

Yes, Kala had met this man before. She watched him run from the Holloton Library as it crumpled beneath orange fires.

"You're not leaving this time," Kala whispered.

She dug her feet into the stage and started running. Then, Kala lifted her father's watch gear high overhead and leaped.

<u>6</u>

I have to keep Mom safe... I'm not ready to be Kindler!

Kala launched herself from the library's stage, wielding a watch gear overhead. Midair, memories bombarded her. Kala remembered a metal man trembling beneath an electric current.... Blood pulsing from his hideous arms.... His leap from atop the yew tree...

I won't let you hurt Mom... Not again!

More memories flooded Kala's sight: a rock that glowed with curious, green light... a bloody path of footprints burned into fresh snow... a pair of empty eyes...

Kala expected to feel the slice of flesh and crunch of bone as she sunk her watch gear into the stranger's chest, but something entirely different happened.

Kala never quite made it into the air. Just before she took flight, her mother swung an arm into her chest and yanked her to the ground.

Kala lay sprawled on the library's stage, where she watched the old man in the crowd. He laughed as a Tynk spun harmlessly between his fingers. He wasn't the metal stranger from the night of the fire. He was no danger at all.

"What's gotten into you?" Luana seethed.

"He was trying to steal Aeverum, and… and I thought he was attacking you!" Kala sputtered. "He looked just like the man I've been telling you about — the one who started the fire!"

"That's Frank. He's a chemist… not some madman from your nightmares," Luana snarled.

Confusion clouded Kala. All her memories of that night, the fire and the metal man, they were all so blurred. Was he real? Or was Kala making it all up?

"I thought he was hurting you," Kala said, her voice shrinking.

"No one's trying to hurt me," Luana said. "For the last time. Your father started that fire and ran away from it — that's all there is to it. These stories you've spun up in your head… You can't believe them, Kala!"

Kala didn't know what to think. Could her mind really betray her like this? Her visions felt so real… And Mortimer wouldn't just run away…

A scream snapped Kala and Luana out of their exchange. In

the middle of the library, Gwen Duckworth was pointing at Colin O'Claire. He lay motionless on the ground, lost in the spin of his Tynk.

"Didn't I warn you about those?" Luana said, but the warning was far too late. Colin was motionless on the ground; his eyes were a blank void.

"He's turned to stone!" Gwen squeeled.

"Yes, I can see that," Luana muttured. Her voice was weak with fatigue. She hobbled over to Colin and kicked his Tynk away. His eyes were nearly empty now, robbed of their light and their vital spark.

Kala recognized that hollow look: it haunted her memories from the night of the fire. She watched her mother let a spark of Aeverum's fire drip from her fingertip down onto Colin's eyes. It reignited their life. His dull grey pupils were refilled with brown and green flares.

"How many fingers am I holding up?" Luana asked him, holding three crooked fingers in front of the boy.

"Where's my Tynk?" Colin gasped, ignoring the question.

"You're worried about the toy?" Luana sputtered.

"Where'd you put it?" Colin asked.

In that moment, Luana realized that her library's stories… Aeverum… they were all nothing compared to the draw of TynkerVille's toys.

"All of you… Get out! Now!"

Luana's voice broke like thunder. She crushed Colin's Tynk beneath her heel as if it were nothing more than a dead leaf.

That's when the children, and Frank the old man, started running. They'd seen blue fire drip from Luana's hands. They'd been knocked over by the power of her voice. Now, they'd watched steel crumble beneath her foot. The children wanted no part of the Kindler's hidden powers, even if she did look old and frail.

Alone with her daughter, Luana's exasperation became palpable. "The next Kindler and you try to stab someone? Where did you get that watch gear, anyway?"

"There was something strange in the fire," Kala insisted.

But Luana glanced up at Aeverum and found the fire serene and unharmed. "You're lying to yourself," she said firmly. "Whatever you thought you saw that night... None of it's real, Kala."

"Fine," Kala sighed. "Whatever you say."

Luana shook her head. "This isn't an ordinary library — don't you realize that? You're the next Kindler. That means no more paranoid delusions. No more hiding from stories. No more cutting open your hand!"

"You saw me do that?"

"Saw you? All you do is poke at that scarred palm." Luana exhaled. "There's fire in you, Kala. You won't find it by digging."

Kala was frightened by her mother's words. She wasn't ready to be Kindler. She hadn't found the blue fire that was supposed to rush through her veins. She couldn't tell stories, much less keep Aeverum burning for the *entire* world.

"I know all that," Kala whispered.

Luana sighed, then picked up the Tynk she'd crushed under her foot. There were dozens of tiny mirrors shattered inside the toy's broken orb.

"These aren't just toys," Luana repeated. "There's something else happening here."

Kala stared into the Tynk's mirrors. She started to get lost in her own broken reflection, until her mother snapped the toy away.

"See?" Luana said. "They trap your eyes."

Kala blushed. Her brain felt a little fuzzy from staring into the Tynk.

"You were coughing before," Kala said. "I saw blood."

Luana waved a hand at Aeverum. "I'm tied to the fire, you know that, Kala. If it shrinks, then I shrink with it. It's all part of being Kindler."

"Well, I don't want you to shrink," Kala said.

Luana grinned and wrinkles twisted all over her face. She was just shy of forty years old but looked much closer to fifty.

"That's why we need you," Luana said. "I've had a good run, Kala. But being Kindler? No, not anymore. We all deserve someone new."

Kala turned down her palms, hiding their scars. "And *someone* means me."

"Can we find your fire?" Luana asked. "There are other ways to do it. You won't have to read a story, I promise."

Kala paused. "We can try," she answered after a long

moment. "Just once."

Luana pressed her hand against the library's yew tree and something brilliant happened. Blue veins appeared in the tree's bark: twisting, turning and rushing to meet their Kindler. The veins all connected up to Aeverum and lit the library in a warm, sapphire glow.

"Your turn," Luana said. "Go ahead, rest your hand on the tree."

Kala hesitated for a moment, then placed her palm against the yew tree. She waited for the same thing to happen to her, for blue fires to rush to her fingertips. She pressed her palm harder against the tree and felt the cut on her hand rip open. She waited... and waited... and waited...

But nothing was happening. No blue veins raced towards Kala. No fires simmered in her palms.

Luana looked over and frowned. "Give me your hands," she said. "I'll bring the fire out. I'm the one who gave it to you, after all."

Kala took her hand off the tree and offered it to her mother. Her right palm was bleeding again.

"You didn't have to cut yourself," Luana whispered.

She sent a tendril of fire down into Kala's hand. It wriggled through her cut and danced up her arm. Kala closed her eyes and felt the warm flame bounce between her ribs, then roll down into her core. It stayed there for a minute or so, searching, then left.

"Is it there?" Kala asked. "You found my fire?"

She opened her eyes, ready to watch blue light dance through her hands. But Kala found her palms bare. They were full of sweat and blood, but nothing more.

"Empty," Luana whispered. "I... I couldn't find anything, Kala."

"So what does that mean?" Kala asked.

"It must be a mistake," her mother answered. "Yes, it's just a mistake."

<u>7</u>

The sun set low outside the Holloton Library. Most of its light was blocked by the center of the city and the massive structures that were recently built there. They were skyscrapers made of wood and glass that reached hundreds of feet into the air.

Luana Blaise stepped into the evening's warm glow and found the wrinkles on her face hidden for just a moment. She looked young, or at least, as she should for her age.

Beside her, Kala turned her melted watch gear through her fingers and thought of her father. Mortimer Blaise was still missing from the night of the fire. Luana had searched for weeks on end but found no sign of him. Mortimer had become a phantom who lived only in the back of Kala's mind.

Lost in thought, neither Kala nor Luana spoke of what happened minutes ago. Was it possible that Kala, the next Kindler, had *no* fire inside her at all?

"There's no one out to get us," Luana murmured softly, more to herself than to Kala.

"There was a hand in the fire," Kala insisted. "I saw it."

"You're still seeing things that aren't there," Luana sighed. "I need you to watch Aeverum tonight."

"Are you going to search for Dad?" Kala asked. Her voice was a mix of hope and desperation. "Can I come with you this time?"

"Start reading stories. That's how you can help," Luana answered.

She walked onto the road. Its dirt was packed tightly by the many caravans that streamed into the center of Holloton, bringing metal ores and workers to shape them.

Kala swept around her mother and looked deep into her eyes. "Just tell me where you're going," she said. "What have you found about Dad?"

Luana nudged her daughter aside. She crossed the road to their home, which sat less than thirty feet from the Holloton Library. The Blaise's house was two stories high and made from wood and glass. It stood on the outskirts of Holloton, closer to the surrounding forest than the city's center. It had a yard of overgrown shrubs and a well with no water in it.

The true glory of the Blaise's home was its windows: they were each positioned to face their partners atop the Holloton

Library. From nearly anywhere in their home, Kala and Luana could see Aeverum, the Kindler's fire.

But Kala wasn't thinking about blue fires now. She was stuck on thoughts of her father.

"Take me with you," Kala said, running ahead of her mother and throwing her arms across their front door. "Just for one night. Maybe I'll see something you can't."

"Move, Kala."

"Why won't you take me?"

"Because you're not a Kindler!" Luana roared. "You don't have your fire, Kala. You'd only get in the way."

"You said there's fire in me," Kala whispered. "Even if it didn't want to come out."

"There is fire, Kala… there has to be." Luana sighed. "But I can't risk you getting hurt. Not now."

Small and flameless, Kala slipped into her home and waited for her mother to follow. But Luana remained outside, and with a wavering hand, started to close their front door.

"I know I'm hard on you," Luana said, then trailed off. "I'll be back soon. Lock the door and watch Aeverum."

Kala rested her palms against an old window and watched her mother walk down the road towards the center of Holloton and TynkerVille. Slumped over her cane, Luana moved anonymously. The caravans that passed knew nothing of her nature. To them, Luana Blaise was just another stranger, not the keeper of Imagination.

"I know I can help you," Kala whispered.

41

Her breath fogged the window, and when the haze cleared, her mother was gone. Already, Luana was swallowed by the cluster of skyscrapers in Holloton's center. These new, wooden towers all shared a common root: TynkerVille. The bustling factory had become Holloton's heartbeat as it slurped in ore and churned out thousands of metal Tynks.

Kala turned away from the buildings and looked around her home. It was smaller in every way. Its first floor had a kitchen lined with old books. Upstairs, there was a simple bedroom that Kala and Luana shared.

There was also a forgotten room tucked beneath a spiral stairway. Hidden behind a locked door, Mortimer Blaise's old workshop lied empty and waiting. The room was filled with heavy watchmaking machines. It was a menagerie of cogs, rotors and tiny jewels.

That's what Kala remembered, at least. She knew where the key to Mortimer's workshop was hidden (behind the cover of her mother's book *The Magic Faucet*) but rarely used it. The room brought memories roaring back. It forced Kala to remember everything that her father's disappearance had stolen away...

Kala lowered her eyes and paced through her kitchen. She found a bowl of sliced peaches with a note on its rim. *Practice your reading*, it said. *Be back soon - Mom.*

Kala tore the note away and watched it flutter down. It began vibrating when it hit the floor as Kala felt a low *hum* drum against her heels. It was a new noise that came from somewhere deep below the ground.

Kala looked outside and saw Aeverum still burning; there was nothing wrong with the blue flame. But beyond the fire, the city of Holloton was coming to life. Its cloud-breaking buildings roared with candlelight, packed full of people and sound. The city seemed to be calling out to Kala, beckoning her.

"Is that where you went, Dad?" Kala whispered.

She looked to her father's workshop and tried to picture the man who once toiled there. But Kala couldn't remember anything that resembled Mortimer. His face had become a ghost that lied just beyond her reach.

Kala curled her hands into fists and sunk her fingers into her wounded palm. "I can help," she said, balling her fists tighter. "I can find you."

She looked around and found her home perfectly still. There was no Kindler roaming its floors; Luana would be gone until late in the night. But outside, the city of Holloton and the jewel at its center, *TynkerVille*, awaited. Still, Kala could feel the hum of the factory thumping against her heels.

She wanted to search for her father.

She wanted to find the fist that wriggled through Aeverum.

She wanted to show her mother she wasn't useless.

Kala took one last look at Aeverum and recalled her mother's words: *Lock the door. Watch the fire.* Then, she clutched her father's watch gear and walked outside.

"I'll find you, Dad. I'll find you if she can't."

43

With her eyes fixed high in the sky, on skyscrapers and roaring candlelight, Kala stepped down the road. For the very first time, she was heading for TynkerVille.

8

Kala's heart skipped a beat as she narrowly dodged a caravan barreling down the road. Its horse reared to a halt and its driver hurled a disapproving glare. He was just one among a sea of drivers, all funneling goods into the center of Holloton.

"Watch where you're going!" the driver barked, his voice rough as gravel.

Kala stepped back and her gaze fell onto the caravan's cargo. It held a rich vein of raw metals, all destined for TynkerVille's machines.

She composed herself and eyed the line of caravans with interest. She focused on one in particular, whose driver had grey, cloudy eyes. As he creaked by, Kala swung herself onto the back of his cart and hitched a silent ride.

"Who's there?" the driver croaked, sensing the disturbance.

He peered back, but his vision failed to register Kala. She was camouflaged on a stack of silver ore.

"Mind the potholes," the old driver muttered to his horse, urging her onward.

Hidden among silver, Kala watched the changing face of Holloton. The quaint homes of the outer city turned into towering wood and glass skyscrapers.

Soon, the cart that carried Kala sputtered to a stop. It sat at the very back of a long line of traffic; the roads to TynkerVille narrowed in this part of the city, so carts could only move in a single file line.

"Thanks," Kala whispered to her driver. She slipped onto the street and sent rocks tumbling against the back of his cart. But this hardly mattered, because everywhere in this part of Holloton, there was sound.

Kala's feet sank into wet dirt as she jumped onto the street. She was struck by a rush of new scents: rotten fruit, old water and sweat, all wound into one powerful smell. Kala inhaled them deeply, drawing Holloton in through her nose.

Her eyes began leaping beyond her control. They were drawn to huge flickers of light that came from signs made from hundreds of candles. One of these signs captured Kala's attention in particular. It said *TynkerVille* in large, royal blue letters. Kala followed the sign a block to the east, where she found a crowd of strangers rushing along a street full of curious shops.

One of these was called TynkerMeals, a store that sold nothing but slender pieces of hollow wood. Customers paid for these batons, opened them from their ends and tipped heaps of chopped-up food down into their throats. These were meals like *The Special Meal* (pounded chicken and pine nuts), *The Fruit Meal* (apples, pears, peaches), and *The Deal Meal* (assorted meats and spices).

Kala gagged as full meals were swallowed in single gulps. She wondered what meat *The Deal Meal* was made from; a gross, pink sludge dripped from those tubes.

Kala turned back to the street and saw its crowd start to shimmer. Their Tynks were all glinting in the light of freshly lit candles. These glimmers pulled Kala deeper into the road. She stumbled over an empty TynkerMeal but didn't stop. She slipped into the crowd and became lost in the shine of whirling Tynks.

But the crowd didn't sweep Kala in as she expected. She was immediately thrown into a harsh current of knees, feet and belt buckles. Kala flailed her arms and struggled to catch her breath. She yelped, hoping someone knocking past her would hear, but the strangers kept crashing into Kala and moving past her.

Within seconds Kala was pushed to the ground, where light fled her. She was consumed by darkness and began gasping for help.

Trapped, Kala felt something seize her arm. It was a small hand with an iron grip.

<u>9</u>

Long, jagged fingernails stabbed at Kala's skin. She was pulled
from the bustling crowd and onto the safety of the road's edge.
Bruises were already purpling on Kala's legs and blood spilled
from her lip.

She looked at the hand, then the person, who saved her. He
was a boy no older than she was, a curious looking one at that.

His hair was like a bird's nest, a jumble of curls that grew
thicker towards the back of his head. He carried a drawstring
bag on the end of a walking stick that jingled with each of his
steps. His shoes were blocks of wood held together with thick
strings.

"Thanks," Kala muttered to the boy, wiping blood from her
lip.

"You don't stop," he said. "Not there."

"I wasn't *trying* to get trampled."

"You're new here, right?"

The boy dipped a hand into his drawstring bag. He pulled out a TynkerMeal, the one with fruit, and dumped it into his mouth.

"You mean new in Holloton?" Kala said. "No, I've lived here my whole life."

"I mean *here*. TynkerVille."

"I thought TynkerVille was a toy factory?" Kala asked.

"They own all this, too. It's all TynkerVille."

The boy swept his hand along the street. Kala saw the endless row of shops and the shimmering Tynks that lit their windows.

"Does everyone have one?" Kala asked. "A Tynk?"

The boy reached inside his shirt and produced a necklace made of string. On its end, hanging like a giant amulet, was a Tynk. With a light flick of his wrist, the boy sent the toy spinning.

"Go on, you hold it," he said.

Keeping the Tynk strapped around his neck, the boy lifted the toy towards Kala. She took it in her hands and felt her chest begin to flutter. The Tynk was lighter than Kala expected, a slender wheel fixed onto a hollow orb. She held it between her thumb and pointer finger and watched it spin without fail, as if a spell were making it immune to friction. The Tynk felt perfect in Kala's hands, crafted just for her fingers.

As the toy spun, Kala watched her face glimmer in the turning steel. She fell into the trance of her own reflection as the Tynk's orb cracked open. Inside, Kala saw dozens of tiny mirrors set into the Tynk's core, and...

"Weird, right?" The boy snapped his Tynk back and stuffed it down his shirt. Immediately, the space between Kala's fingers felt painfully empty.

"Ten seconds, that's the trick," the boy went on. "Look any longer and you get *drained*."

""Drained?" Kala said. "Can... can I see it again?"

"No, you cannot."

The boy lifted his walking stick, and the drawstring bag on its end, back over his shoulder. He turned from Kala and walked away. "Just keep moving when you're in the crowd," he called. "If you can't do that, you don't belong here!"

The boy dipped effortlessly into the rush of strangers and vanished. Kala looked for some sign of him—a wave of his shirt, a bounce of his curly hair—and found nothing. But, not four seconds later, the boy popped back onto the side of the road and marched towards Kala. There was a hazel flicker in his eye.

"What's your name?" he shouted.

"Kala. Kala Blaise."

"I'm Fin. Just Fin."

Fin lifted his fingers towards Kala. They were coated with grime, like they'd been trapped between the cogs of an old machine. Kala let Fin's hand waver in the air. She did not shake

50

it.

"You want a Tynk, don't you?" Fin asked, pulling back his hand.

The question startled Kala. Of course she wanted a Tynk, but what would her mother think?

"Maybe," she said. "I might want one."

"What's it worth to you?"

Fin tapped his foot, making squishing sounds in the dirt. Kala struggled for an answer, then began patting down her jacket. There were all sorts of items stowed in its pockets, but no money.

"I don't have much," Kala sighed.

Fin shook his stick and made its drawstring bag jingle. "I don't need money. I'm more interested in *curiosities*."

"You mean stuff?" Kala said. "Oh, I've got lots of stuff."

She lifted her arms and revealed the pockets she'd sewn into the fabric of her jacket.

"What about paper? I bet that's hard to find here," Kala said, pulling out a bundle of shredded notes. "How about charcoal nubs? Candle wax?"

Useless items flew from Kala's coat and made a heap at her feet. Her hands kept rifling through her jacket, but she was careful not to open the pocket that held her father's old watch gear. Kala would not part with that.

"Stop," Fin said, a mad twinkle in his eye. "I know what I want."

"The paper, right? Charcoal's cheap, you can find it—"

51

"The coat."

"The coat?" Kala wrapped her arms protectively around herself. "You can't have it. The coat's mine."

"I know that," Fin said. "And I've never seen one like it. That's why I want it."

Fin held out his hand again. His Tynk bobbed beneath his shirt, drawing Kala's eyes.

"I'll sweeten the deal," Fin said. "You won't get my Tynk… you'll get a *brand new* one. They're releasing the new models tonight and I know where they'll be. I'll get you to the front of the line. All I need is that coat."

Kala bowed towards the hunk of metal poking out from Fin's shirt. She wanted that feeling again, the Tynk spinning perfectly between her fingers.

"Fine," she said. "Take the coat, just not the stuff inside."

"Fair enough."

Kala emptied her coat onto the ground. She thought about breaking the deal she'd just made, she *really* loved that coat, but something more powerful kept her lips sealed. It was a phantom feeling in her hands, a metallic spin between her fingers.

Sewing needles, scraps from old books, a handful of oats and other objects formed a tower on the ground. On top of this pile, Kala rested her father's melted watch gear. It caught TynkerVille's lights just like the Tynks did. It glimmered up at Fin.

"What is *that?*" Fin asked. He reached down, but Kala batted his hand away.

"It's from my father," Kala answered, stowing the gear away. "He made watches."

"Good ones, I bet. I've never seen an edge like that on a rotor."

"Yeah, he was good."

"*Was* good... What about now?"

Kala shoved her coat into Fin's arms. "Tell me where we're going."

"I asked you a question."

"You got the coat, that was the deal. Where's my Tynk?"

"Stubborn," Fin sighed. "Follow me."

Fin slipped on Kala's coat and sifted his hands through its pockets. Satisfied with his trade, he led Kala down the long row of shops. Eight blocks to the north, Fin turned down a slender alleyway. It was much darker than the main road, lit by a smattering of dim candles.

"Keep your eyes on me," Fin said, stepping into the dark. "*Only* me."

Kala could hardly see two feet in front of her. She saw Fin step over something on the ground and realized it was a person: a perfectly still woman was propped up against the wall. Her face was mute and her eyes were clouded with a grey haze.

There were more people like her. All of them were still. All of them had milky eyes.

"What are they?" Kala whispered.

53

"I said not to look," Fin hissed. "They're people. Same as you and me."

"What's wrong with their eyes?"

Fin waved a hand at one of the alley-dwellers. She was breathing but couldn't see the hand moving in front of her. She looked something like Colin O'Claire when he collapsed in the library.

"They're drained," Fin whispered. "Stared into Tynks too long. TynkerVille hides them when it happens. No one knows where they take them."

Kala looked down at the grey-eyed woman. There was no fire burning behind her eyes, no spark that lit her mind. "She's empty."

"Just forget it," Fin snarled. "We're not far away. Keep following me."

Kala marched on over the legs of drained strangers and around puddles of filth. She grew confused, and wanted to know where Fin's sudden anger came from. She also wanted to know what was really inside his jingling, drawstring bag.

When the pair reached the end of the alley, Kala grabbed Fin by the shoulder and spun him around. "Why are you doing this?" she asked.

"I like your coat," Fin said. "And my bag's getting full. I need the extra room."

"No, I mean why did you save me? You could have just left me in the road."

Fin shrugged. "Because I remember my first time in

54

TynkerVille."

Fin walked onto the well-lit edge of the main road. This new street was filled with more bizarre shops, and above them all, more wooden homes were stacked high in the air.

"So do you live in one of those?" Kala asked, nodding at the windows high above them.

"Not anymore," Fin sighed. "Come on, we're almost there."

He and Kala walked past more curious shops. There was Tynk-o-Wager, TynkerAles and TynkerCaps, a store that sold wired caps that could suspend your Tynk right in front of your face. Fin stopped three streets down from there and slouched against the window of a dark, run-down store.

"What's this?" Kala asked.

"This is it. Where they're selling the new Tynks," Fin said. Above him, a rusted sign read *TynkerTales*. "They sold books for a while," Fin went on. "Never caught on."

"This doesn't look like a Tynk store."

"They'll be here," Fin said, a grin creeping over his lips. "You'll see, Kala."

10

Kala began tapping her foot so Fin could hear it squishing in the dirt. She thought of her parents and realized she didn't have time to wait around for metal toys. Was Kala's father really lost somewhere in Holloton's maze of wooden buildings? If he was, where would Kala even begin to look? And where was Luana? Would she be heading home soon, expecting to find Kala fast asleep?

"Look Fin, I don't have all night," Kala muttered.

"Just wait one minute," Fin grumbled. "Be a *little* patient."

Kala let out a humph and folded her arms across her chest. She expected to feel the warmth of her olive coat, but that was gone, traded for the chance to stand outside of this filthy building. Kala was starting to think she lost her trade with Fin.

"If you're trying to trick me," Kala said, "I'll take my coat right back… and I'll take your bag, too!"

"Would you just be quiet?" Fin hissed. "You're not—"

His mouth kept moving, but Kala couldn't hear any of Fin's words. That's because an eruption of sound filled Holloton's air. It was a burst of noise that collapsed into words, and then, into a voice. It brought the city's crowds to a halt. At last, they looked up from their Tynks.

Good evening, Kala heard through muffled ears. *Tonight, we release Tynk Two.*

This voice didn't come from a mouth. It bounced off walls, boomed from lampposts and screamed down TynkerVille's skyscrapers. It came from everywhere all at once.

In six minutes, a new era of entertainment will begin, the voice went on. *But first, an announcement… Every person who purchases a Tynk Two will be entered into the Tour of TynkerVille sweepstakes. The winners will experience a one-day tour of TynkerVille, the first and **only** of its kind. Winners will also create a Tynk of their own and work alongside TynkerVille's Designer.*

Applause crashed through Holloton, and Kala couldn't help but share the crowd's excitement. A Tynk of her own design with her name, *Kala Blaise,* etched into its steel… who wouldn't want one of those?

The Tynk Two will startle some of you. We ask that you trust in TynkerVille. We know what you want. Let us show you.

Kala searched for the source of the towering voice. It seemed to be coming from many points above her, leaping out from

57

thin slivers of wood. These slices of sound met and multiplied in Holloton's streets, as if the city's buildings themselves were speaking.

Tynk Two will be available for sale starting at 9:47pm tonight. It will cost one silver and four tins, or any equivalent combination of goods.

More people began whisking into the road. They wore grey jumpsuits with TynkerVille *T's* sewn onto the middle of their chests. They slipped into the old bookstore behind Kala, locked the door behind them, and began removing piles of trash with copper shovels.

...47 Marcator Avenue will have a limited supply, and so will 23 Montinary Boulevard...

There was a massive shuffle of bodies as the everywhere-voice listed the locations where new Tynks would be sold. The people in the road scrambled awkwardly, all trying to figure out where the nearest Tynk Two would be available.

Amidst the chaos, Fin grabbed Kala's wrist and held up his palm. *Wait right here,* Fin mouthed, and pulled Kala right up to the locked door of TynkerTales so that they were just inches from its glass.

...33 Pikatally Lane will have a few, and lastly, so will 12 Caverness Lane. We remind you to be a neighbor, in every sense of the word, when purchasing your Tynk Two. Good day.

The voice disappeared and all Kala could hear was the rush of the crowds around her.

"Stay close to me!" Fin shouted. "Take a deep breath... use

your nails if you have to!"

A crush of people slammed into Kala and Fin and squeezed them against the glass door of TynkerTales. Through gaps in their flailing limbs, Kala could see a string of letters on the bookshop's window. *33 Pikatally Lane*. Fin was right: Tynk Two's would be sold here.

Moments later, candles roared to life inside the old bookstore. All the trash and books were gone. In their place were three giant blocks of cherry-colored wood, each fixed onto the back wall of TynkerTales.

Kala struggled to keep her sight on the old bookstore. She was smothered by a swarm of strangers, squeezed against TynkerTales so harshly that air was pushed right out of her lungs. Kala's vision started to speckle. Gasping, she felt fingernails rake at her skin as the fists of strangers smacked the side of her head.

But as Kala's vision blackened, the door behind her gave way. She spilled into TynkerTales and heaved in a gasp of fresh air. Beside Kala, Fin smiled after a long breath of his own. They were both bloody and lightheaded. They were both first in line for a Tynk Two.

"We're okay now," Fin said, helping Kala to her feet. "They won't sell to anyone who pushes inside their stores. It's one of TynkerVille's rules."

Silently, Kala watched the crowd outside. They were mad: clawing each other and doing all they could to reach the front of the growing line. But when they entered TynkerTales, each of the strangers grew perfectly still. It was like the shop had magic whistling through it. Quietly, three spellbound lines formed, one in front of each block of cherry wood.

Kala was first up on the left line. A few feet away, Fin stepped into TynkerTales' middle row. They both moved slowly towards the cubes of wood ahead of them.

"Fin, I don't have any money," Kala whispered.

"You heard them," Fin said, "a silver and four, *or equivalent.* Give them your dad's watch gear, it's worth twice that much!"

"No way!" Kala hissed. "I can't give them that. Do they take anything else?"

"Nothing that you've got. They don't need string and paper. TynkerVille wants metal," Fin said. He reached the cherry-colored block at the end of his row. He placed his palm on the wood and moved its front panel to the side. A small room was revealed that took up half of the cube's interior.

"Come on. You know you want one, Kala," Fin said.

He stepped into the cherry cube and closed its front panel behind him. He left Kala alone in a room full of strangers. Standing before her own cube of polished wood, Kala started to shiver. She reached into her pocket and felt her father's watch gear. It was a perfect, melted crescent that stilled her trembling hands. It was a piece of her father and the past they once shared. Kala thought of backwards clocks and complicated wristwatches. She thought of Mortimer Blaise.

"Come on," someone stammered behind Kala. "*Move it.*"

The air in TynkerTales grew warm as the strangers behind

Kala started shuffling their feet. They were impatient, looming above her and breathing down her neck. Kala decided she didn't need any more battles with the city's crowds, and so, like Fin did before, she pressed her hand against the center of the wooden cube and pushed. With ease, the cube's front panel slid open and revealed a small room. Kala stepped inside and found a lone candle and two compartments that were carved into the cube's wall.

One said *Tynk*. The other said *Payment*.

The wooden panel snapped closed behind Kala, leaving her totally alone. The only thing left to comfort her was the melted gear in her hands. Instinctively, Kala turned her father's watch gear through her fingers.

"Name," a muffled voice said. It came through the wall of the cube and Kala realized there was another hollow room beside her.

"Kala Blaise."

"And you are here for a Tynk Two?"

Kala looked down, considering her answer. She saw her father's watch gear catch the light from the room's lone candle. It shimmered brilliantly and made Kala think of the lump beneath Fin's shirt. That awesome whirl of metal… yes, Kala needed to have a Tynk.

"I want one," she whispered.

Kala was gripped by the spin of Fin's Tynk, even though it left her fingers long ago. She lifted her hand towards the compartment that said *Payment* and dropped her father's watch gear inside. An instant later, a gloved hand swiped the gear away before Kala could realize what she'd done.

"Hey, I didn't mean that!" Kala yelled, pounding on the wall. "Give it back!"

No one answered Kala, but there was a soft thud that came from the cube's other compartment. Something fell into the *Tynk* cubby: a small wooden box and two silver coins.

"I don't want those!" Kala shouted. "I want my watch gear!"

Kala tried to throw the wooden box back up the cubby. But every time she tossed it up, the box came tumbling back down. Eventually, a crack opened at one of its corners. Through this splinter in the wood, Kala saw the glint of steel.

She pried open the wooden box and found a brand new Tynk Two. It was like the Tynk that hung from Fin's neck, but much finer. Instead of a simple sphere, this Tynk Two had twin metal wheels that flew around a central steel orb. Kala placed two of her fingers on the points where these wheels met and flicked her wrist.

The Tynk set in motion. Its wheels flashed in opposite directions, spinning around each other and creating a phantom globe around the steel ball they were connected to. It created a circle within a flickering circle.

Kala fell deeply into the metal haze in her hands. She traced each of the Tynk's pieces and saw the finely machined points that joined them. She didn't feel the ground beneath her start to tilt and hardly noticed as she was dumped onto the road behind TynkerTales.

This new street was totally silent; everyone here had a new Tynk. The road grew crowded as TynkerTales dumped more customers onto it. Kala didn't pay these other people any attention, including Fin, who was standing just a few feet away from her.

Both were staring into the spinning metal in their hands. Their new Tynks were opening now, revealing hundreds of tiny mirrors that lined their inner cores. Kala and Fin were transfixed by their own reflections as they drifted away from each other. They stumbled into thin alleyways and were lost to darkness.

There were no goodbyes. Only new Tynks.

11

Kala's vision was a blur of steel and mirrors. Stumbling into a dark alley, she tripped over the strangers who were already lying there. Kala moved past them and settled beneath a dim candle. In its weak light, she watched her Tynk spin.

Time dripped away. The new Tynk was a perfect machine, and for many minutes, it spun without stopping. Whenever it started to slow, Kala gave her wrist another flick and sent the Tynk whirring once more.

Glimmering metal. Rings of flickering wheels. Dozens of mirrors and their tiny reflections. These became Kala's world... After a timeless spell, Kala's trance was broken by a cramp in her foot. She placed her Tynk inside her pocket and ran a thumb over her heel. It eased the pain and made Kala look around and see what lay around her.

She gasped.

Twenty empty-eyed strangers were huddled around the alley's candlelight. They moaned as spit trickled from their mouths. They were the *drained*, the people who'd stared into Tynks for too long and were now forgotten by their city.

Kala had to admit, her mind did feel a little fuzzy after looking at the Tynk Two. It was like something vital had slipped away without her knowing it...

She saw a sliver of moonlight along the wall and realized she had no idea what time it was. How long had she been staring at her Tynk? All Kala could remember was a haze of steel.

"Mom," Kala whispered.

Her stomach knotted as she thought of her mother. Kala had never left home for this long before. If Luana found out, Kala's punishment would be huge.

Frantic, Kala stumbled back onto one of Holloton's wider main roads. Even this time of night, there were dozens of caravans clopping towards the city's center.

Kala moved opposite of these carts, away from TynkerVille and towards the outskirts of Holloton. She started jogging as thoughts of her mother danced through her head. Undoubtedly, Luana Blaise would be stomping through their kitchen waiting for Kala to return.

Watch the fire... Read! Kala thought, turning her mother's words through her mind.

She stumbled south as Holloton's skyscrapers shrunk back into two and three-story homes. At last, Kala could see the fullness of the sky. There was a bright bloom of light growing in the east. Morning was coming.

Kala's lungs burned as she wound through countless more streets. She reeked of sweat and TynkerVille, but there was nothing she could do about that now. She came to a stop outside her family's library and exhaled with relief when she saw its blue flame still simmering away atop the yew tree.

But now would come the real test. Kala crossed the road and pressed an ear to the front door of her home. She expected to hear her mother pacing inside but didn't hear any such sounds. Confused, Kala cracked open the door. There was nothing but silence inside. There was no movement in the kitchen, nor on the home's spiral staircase. Tip-toeing upstairs, Kala found the second floor empty, too.

"Mom?" Kala whispered. "Are you here?"

There was no sign that Luana had ever returned home. In fact, nothing had moved since Kala left. Her mother would have no idea she ever went to TynkerVille.

Kala sighed and felt strength leave her body. She realized she was impossibly tired, impossibly filthy and impossibly bruised. Despite all this, she sensed something heavy building in the back of her mind. It was a cloud of guilt whose source was tucked beneath a spiral stairwell: Mortimer Blaise's workshop, locked and silent.

That's what Kala forgot. She went to TynkerVille in search

of her father but came back with nothing more than a metal toy. She'd even given away her father's watch gear in trade.

Kala drifted downstairs and stepped underneath the stairway. She curled her fingers around the cold knob of her father's workshop and pulled. It hardly budged. But Kala knew where her mother kept its key, and a minute later, she twisted the workshop's door open.

Dust rushed out. Light trickled in.

Kala found a box of matches and struck one. The ember gave off a small crescent of warmth, until Kala lowered the flame onto a wick and illuminated her father's workshop.

Kala smiled at one of her father's earliest inventions, a glass orb that could multiply the light of a candle. Alight, it allowed Kala to see the clutter of metal and wood inside the workshop: half-finished watch gears and drawings of those that never came to be.

Kala picked up a piece of oily cloth with faded, charcoal drawings scribbled on it. It was a picture of a horribly complex machine that Mortimer had labeled a *Jumping Hands Chronograph*.

"Is that what you were working on?" Kala asked.

She let the cloth slip through her fingers and felt her chin start to quake. Kala couldn't hold back her tears any longer. She collapsed into a heap and cried while her father's inventions glistened around her.

"You didn't even look for him," Kala mumbled.

She pulled a hunk of metal down from one of the

workshop's shelves. It was a watch movement made of tiny gears, and with two fingers, Kala plucked away its steel rotor. It was just like the gear she'd sold to TynkerVille.

"Where'd you go, Dad?" Kala whispered. "You can come back now, okay?"

Kala noticed something underneath one of the workshop's tables. It was a curious book, unlike any of the ones Luana kept in the library. It was a hunk of floppy leather stuffed full of roughly cut pages. It was homemade, from the looks of it.

Kala pulled the book onto her lap. She blew dirt off its cover and revealed a lone, etched word: *Memories*. On the book's first page, there was an inscription written in flowing script: *Here lies a life in pieces. If you are not Mortimer Blaise, this is not your book.*

Kala ignored this warning and began turning over pages. She realized this was far more than just a journal, it was a scrapbook of Mortimer's past. There were sketches of objects — a shiny rattle, a blanket beneath the shade of a blue-flamed tree — paired with long, illegible passages written by Mortimer.

There were items fastened to the pages, too. Kala found a lock of her infant hair and an old drawing she had made of her family. The figures were formed with wobbly lines. The names listed below their linked hands were *Dad*, *Me* and *Mom*.

"You kept everything," Kala whispered.

On one of the scrapbook's pages, about two thirds of the way through, Kala found an object that made her stop. It was a small sliver of iron lashed down with twine.

Kala ran her finger over the coarse metal. She remembered her father's hand atop hers, guiding an iron block through a churning saw. Kala and Mortimer had made this chunk of metal together, long ago.

If you love something, make it in metal, a familiar voice spoke in Kala's mind.

One by one, Kala unraveled the strings that bound the iron. When the piece was free, she brought the iron to her chest and flushed its cold weight against her ribs. It slowed Kala's heartbeat to a dull thump.

Keeping the iron pressed to her skin, Kala kept turning through her father's memory book. As pages tumbled over, as Kala neared the end of the scrapbook, she saw a change in her father's entries. There were no more chronicles of the Blaise family this deep in the book. There were sketches of complex watch gears, instead.

Made with fine black ink, these slender drawings dominated the end of the scrapbook. Cogs, gears and rotors came together into new kinds of watch movements. *Annual Calendar*, one of the drawings was titled. *Leap Year Jump Movement*, another one said.

"What happened to you?" Kala whispered.

Turning wildly through the book's final pages, she watched her father's sketches grow more and more complicated. Watch movements that were once supposed to track seconds and minutes were now tasked with following moonphases and calculating the tilt of the earth's axis.

Mortimer's final drawing was a horrible mash of metal. Incomplete and terrible, it was surrounded by long strings of unreadable scribbles. Kala thought she'd seen this machine somewhere before, but couldn't remember where. Like many things, it was lost somewhere in her mind.

There were no drawings after that. Mortimer's scrapbook was left unfinished when he disappeared. Kala closed the book and clutched the iron in her hand, still warm from the beat of her heart. She pictured an impossible steel machine, the last entry in her father's journal.

Then, as sunlight crept through the windows, weariness finally took Kala. She tucked her father's scrapbook beneath her head and fell asleep on the workshop floor.

<u>12</u>

Kala woke up later that morning in a puddle of drool. She was surprised to find her father's scrapbook tucked beneath her head. She had slept so deeply she didn't remember using it as a pillow.

Kala tucked the scrapbook away and reached into her pocket. She smiled as her fingers curled around the heavy, iron rotor she'd forged with her father years before.

"I'll never give you away," Kala whispered.

From her other pocket, Kala took out her new Tynk. She found the seam that ran along its inner orb and twisted it open. Inside, Kala found a maze of mirrors and cogs that made the Tynk spin perfectly. There was a small, rounded space - a cage of sorts - within these gears. Kala dropped her iron rotor into this space and watched it nestle perfectly into the center of the Tynk. It was an iron heart, made by Kala and Mortimer's hands.

"See? Now, I can't give you away," Kala said.

She squinted as morning light crept deeper into the workshop. Kala wondered where her mother was; Luana often ventured late into the night, but she always returned home. Kala decided to lock her father's workshop and cross the road to the Holloton Library. Maybe Luana was waiting for her there.

"Mom?" Kala shouted. "Are you in here?"

Her voice bounced around the empty library. But there was no one else there, only the yew tree and its blue flame. Kala shrugged and figured her mother would be back sometime in the afternoon. With nothing better to do, she began her daily chores.

Cleaning bookshelves... reordering sections of stories... watching her new Tynk spin... these were the things that kept Kala busy. Only one other person entered the library all morning, a caravan driver in search of a bathroom.

It was not until late in the afternoon that the library's doors cracked open a second time. Luana Blaise hobbled into the library. She had bloody cuts all over her arms and legs.

"Mom!" Kala gasped. "Who did this?"

Luana let out a low wheeze. She slouched against the wall, threw back her head and coughed up blood. There were more cuts on Luana's face, deep and freshly made.

"Who did this?" Kala repeated. She ran for water as her mother sank further into the ground.

"You and I need to talk," Luana wheezed. "Right now. Up there."

Her eyes flittered up towards Aeverum.

"Not now, you can't even walk!" Kala said.

But her mother leaned into her cane and rose.

"There's not much time," Luana said. "Let's go, Kala. Up!"

Kala ran ahead of her mother and climbed the yew tree. Looking behind her, she was surprised to see how easily Luana kept up.

"I've been up this tree a few times myself," Luana said. "We're not as different as you think, Kala."

But as she stepped up the yew tree, Luana revealed more of her wounded face. Kala could see the burnt wrinkles that scored her mother's skin and the cuts that ran over them. Luana slowed as she neared the top of the tree. Her breath became a thick wheeze as fresh blood seeped from her wounds.

"Mom, who hurt you?" Kala asked.

"Look at the fire, Kala. It's all that matters now." Luana rose to the yew tree's highest point and met Aeverum. She moved a hand into the flame and began wriggling her fingers. Aeverum didn't burn Luana. Instead, it listened to its Kindler and sparks of light twinkled in the flame's blue core.

Luana turned her hand and made Aeverum rush around its spindle of wood. She kept manipulating the flame until it

73

became a flat, spinning ring.

"I know you miss your father," Luana said, sighing deeply. "And I think you were right. I found signs. I think your father was taken. He didn't start the fire that night."

"Signs?" Kala said. "What signs?"

"There's something we need to talk about first."

"Something else? What could be more—"

Kala went silent as her mother scooped a piece of Aeverum into her palms and blew air between her hands. The ancient flame rushed outwards and became a thousand blue, fiery ribbons. They wavered through the library like magic threads.

"We need to talk about this," Luana said. "It's all that matters now."

"What are they?" Kala asked. She tapped one of the blue ribbons and felt it bristle against her skin.

"Every thread is a person," Luana said. "They're all people."

She poked a few of the ribbons and they glistened out to their ends.

"Kindlers don't just keep Aeverum going," Luana went on. "We give small pieces of the fire to every living person. Whenever someone's born, they get their own fire from a Kindler. Me, your grandmother and your great-grandmother before her... for thousands of years, the Blaise women have given the world Imagination."

Kala saw that the blue ribbons reached farther than she had first imagined. They seemed endless, flowing to the edges of the library and out through its windows. Unlike the fire months ago, these ribbons didn't burn anything that they touched.

"Everyone deserves Imagination," Luana said. "Even if they waste it watching toys spin."

Kala blushed and placed a hand over her pocket. She made sure her Tynk was tucked safely out of sight. "But what if Imagination does bad things to you?" she asked.

"Who put that idea in your head?" Luana clenched her fist and her system of blue ribbons came racing back in. They collapsed back into Aeverum and reunited the original flame. "I need to show you something and you *need* to listen, Kala. Even if you want to stop me, just please listen."

"What's this all about?" Kala asked.

Luana took a slow and deep breath. She looked up from Aeverum and met her daughter's eyes.

"You're going to be Kindler," Luana said. "Much sooner than either of us thought."

<u>13</u>

Luana used her hands to keep speaking. She moved her fingers into Aeverum, and with a calm stretch of her palms, spread the blue flame. Then, she let sapphire sparks trickle from the tips of her fingers. They merged into an image: a group of children telling stories around a fire.

"For as long as people could speak, they've been telling stories," Luana said. "They're essential, like water and air. Imagine, Kala, that your life is a cup of tea."

"Tea?"

"Tea, that's right. Right now, you're full of flavor: cinnamon, apple skin, maybe a dribble of honey," Luana went on. "But there are some people who want to take all of that away."

Luana's image morphed into something new. The children

around the fire stopped telling stories. Their laughter fell away as they looked into their hands. There, Tynks were spinning. Staring into these metal toys, the children started losing the flames that lit their minds. It vanished through their eyes in a grey smoke.

"The drained. They've let their fires vanish. These people have no Imagination left at all." Luana looked up. "I think that's what the Tynks are really for, Kala."

Kala remembered what Fin had said about the drained. She remembered seeing them strewn about in Holloton's dark alleyways. But was TynkerVille really doing that to people on purpose?

Kala started to ask this very question, but remembered she couldn't give away any knowledge of TynkerVille. Her mother could not know she'd bought a Tynk.

"The drained?" Kala asked. "I've never heard of those before."

"Don't be smart, I know you've seen them," Luana quipped. "TynkerVille's smell takes weeks to wash off."

Kala felt her cheeks burn. Her secret had lasted all of thirty seconds.

"That's not important right now," Luana went on. "Look around, Kala. This library doesn't just keep words on paper. Its stories will live on long after we're gone. They'll carry messages into the future… A grandmother might even speak to her granddaughter this way."

Luana reached down for a particularly dusty book. She

handed it to Kala, who brushed its cover clean. *Quintessa Blaise,* it said. Kala eased the book open and saw words written by her grandmother's hand. She heard a voice stirring within the pages, a forgotten woman narrating the story, making it alive once more.

"Who would want to take this away?" Kala asked.

"Someone who wants control," Luana answered. "The Tynks are a start, but I think there's something much bigger at work. The people who want to take Aeverum from you and me are working on something more sinister than metal toys."

"You mean someone wants to steal our fire?" Kala asked.

"Even more than that. I think these same people took your father. They're using him for their plan and we need to figure out how."

Kala backed away from her mother. She thought of the new Tynk in her pocket and the watch gears that filled Mortimer's workshop. Their shine... their curves... all so similar. How could she not have put it together?

"How long have you known?" Kala whispered.

"That your father might be in TynkerVille? I only just put it together."

"So I've been stuck watching this fire, while Dad's trapped in that city?" Kala asked. "What are they doing with him? I know Dad and he wouldn't make Tynks if they hurt people!"

"I don't know what they're doing to your father," Luana said. The calm in her face broke. "But I'm the world's Kindler. My responsibility is much greater than looking for a man who can't be found. I have to protect myself from the people who want to destroy *me!* TynkerVille is coming, and if they get what they want it will be only you left, Kala. Are you ready for that? Are you ready to guard this fire and keep the world from being drained?"

"You know I'm empty," Kala whispered. "Aeverum will go out if I'm alone."

"Of course you're not empty," Luana said. "You're a Blaise daughter and that means you have fire. But you'll never find it if you don't want it!"

"How do you know I don't want it?"

"How do I know?" Luana shouted. "You've never told a story, not once! You won't even read!"

"That's got nothing to do with—"

"It has everything to do with it! You're afraid of being a Kindler, it's as obvious as—"

"So what if I am!" Kala shouted back. "Ever since I could talk that's all you've said to me. *Kala, it's time to read… One day you'll be me... Kala, you have the fire...* What if I don't want to be Kindler? What if I just want to be *me?"*

Luana sighed. "You don't have a choice," she answered. "It's the only way we'll keep Aeverum burning. Sometimes we have to become what we want least. It's not for us to decide."

"What if I say no? What if I don't care about what I *have* to be?"

Again, Luana answered with her hands. She recreated an image in Aeverum. This time, it was TynkerVille. A herd of

79

drained strangers marched through the city's narrow streets. Each of them was captured by the Tynks in their hands. Together, they were a mass of empty flesh.

"This is what we'll become," Luana said. "No more stories to pass down. No one to hear your grandmother's words. Imagination will bleed right out from our ears. Can you live with that?"

Kala showed her scarred palms to her mother. "I've been looking," she said. "I promise, there's no fire!"

"There is and now you have to find it!"

As Luana spoke, the library's doors sounded a heavy knock. Then, they crackled open. Luana's face twisted with fear as Aeverum shriveled into a tiny ember.

"Get in the tree roots," Luana said.

"What is it, Mom?"

"It's the man who stole your father," Luana breathed. "In the roots, Kala. Now!"

Kala saw worry crawl over her mother's scarred face, then scurried down the side of the yew tree. She settled in the roots and looked up at her mother. Luana Blaise stared ahead and let a ball of blue fire simmer in her palm.

This was the last thing Kala saw. She tucked herself deep into the yew tree's roots and listened. All she could hear were footsteps. Heavy, lonely footsteps.

14

There were horrible clangs of metal and swishes of blue fire. Kala heard falling branches and tumbling leather books. These sounds continued for a long spell and were followed by a longer quiet.

Then, the sound of broken wood snapped through the library. It was followed by the slow wilt of a dying yew tree. Kala looked up from the tree roots and saw chaos. The library's yew tree was destroyed; most of its limbs had been snapped clean in two.

"That's pretty good, Kindler," a low voice spoke. "Not so weak, are you?"

"Aeverum stays here," Luana answered.

The crash of metal and flame resumed, and for the first time,

Kala crept out from the tree roots to see what was happening. Luana Blaise looked as lethal as Kala had ever seen her. She wielded a whip of blue fire, swirling it overhead, then lashing it down on bookstands and tree roots. This fiery, blue rope broke the Holloton Library as it tried to bring down a man in a billowing grey cloak.

He was a stranger with short grey hair and silver barbs rushing up his neck. They were made of metal and wound deep into the stranger's skin. Seeing him stirred something deep in Kala's mind, but she couldn't remember what.

"This would be easier if you put that fire away," the stranger said. "I don't want to hurt you, Kindler."

Luana answered by bringing her whip right down onto the metal man. But the flame bounced off him without leaving so much as a scratch. Angered, the stranger leapt towards Luana and struck her down with an inhuman blow.

"Don't touch her!"

A shout leapt from Kala's mouth, and without thinking, she pressed her palms against the yew tree. She searched for the blue fire that coursed through its veins, but felt nothing, not in her hand or in the tree's bark.

"Why won't you help me?" Kala asked, pounding her fist against the tree. Her new Tynk fell from her pocket and rolled to a stop a few feet away from Luana.

"You bought a Tynk?" Luana whispered. "Get back, Kala. Back in the roots!"

Luana struggled to her feet and stumbled towards her

daughter. The metal stranger didn't stop her at first; he stared at Kala and winced beneath a mysterious rush of pain. But after a moment, the stranger recovered and turned his gaze back towards Luana.

"Take Aeverum… run!" Luana cried, dragging herself across the floor. "You have fire in you Kala. You're ready to be Kindler!"

The stranger's arm moved quickly. It struck Luana with a savage blow that sent her crumbling. Unconscious, she was tossed over the stranger's shoulder and carried towards the library's doors.

"Let go of her!" Kala screamed.

But both she and the stranger knew she was no threat. Kala watched her unmoving mother get carried out of the Holloton Library as a crackling noise sounded somewhere above. It was a tree branch that broke away from the yew tree and toppled down onto Kala.

Darkness consumed Kala. The last things she saw were a metal stranger and a broken Kindler.

15

The Holloton Library was destroyed.

Stacks of books were now heaps of rubble. Windows had erupted into thousands of glass shards that twinkled along the ground. Worst of all, the library's yew tree was devastated. Many of its limbs were hacked away, and at the very top of the tree, a small blue ember was all that remained. The rest of Aeverum had been stolen by the metal stranger.

When Kala woke up, her vision was a blur of light and broken tree limbs. There was a tremendous thump at the sides of her skull. The pain came from a large gash that dripped blood into her hair. Touching this wound, Kala remembered: a man with metal veins… her mother and father, both stolen.

"Mom?" Kala cried. "Come back… come back!"

Her breath was short and crackling and Kala felt a vast emptiness open inside her. Both of her parents, and most of Aeverum, were now gone. The only thing Kala had left was the Tynk that lay a few feet from her. It was the toy that betrayed her mother, distracting Luana long enough for the metal stranger to strike her down.

Kala rose to her feet, scooped up her Tynk, and tried running from the library. Her sight quaked and she wobbled from side to side, but when she burst through the library's doors, she screamed.

"Luana Blaise! Has anyone seen her?"

At first, Kala was blinded by the sun. When her sight sharpened, she saw a family in a caravan awkwardly staring her way. They were drawn by two horses and lurched past Kala without a word.

"Has anyone seen the Kindler?" Kala kept shouting. "What about a man in a grey cloak?"

The strangers passing in the road saw a young girl in tattered clothes screaming blindly at the wind. Kala knew this, but didn't care. Her mother was hurt and stolen, and worse, most of Aeverum was taken.

Kala grew queasy from the wound on her head and stumbled back into the Holloton Library. There, guilt washed over her. The world was going to lose Imagination, and it was all her fault. Kala looked up to what was left of Aeverum.

"I hate you," she scowled. "You know that, right?"

The small flame simmered quietly.

"Mom always said you were living," Kala said. "Well, go ahead. If you're alive, then say something!"

Still, Aeverum was silent.

"Why won't you help me?" Kala shouted. "You never helped me!"

She climbed the broken yew tree until she was just inches from Aeverum. Kala stared at the blue fire and tried to pierce it with her eyes.

"Let me hold you," Kala said. She moved her hand towards the fire, but Aeverum bent around it. Confused, Kala clenched her fingers around the blue flame and watched it slip right through her hands.

"Fine. We can try a different way," Kala huffed. She reached into her pocket, pulled out her new Tynk and, with a flick of her wrist, sent it spinning. "This is why you're dying. You know that, right?"

Kala thrust her toy into Aeverum and watched its metal flash inside the blue flame. Aeverum started rotating, until the blue fire matched the spin of the Tynk.

Startled, Kala let go of her Tynk and watched it hover in the blue fire. Aeverum was spinning wildly, and soon, it swallowed the metal toy in a cyclone of sapphire light.

As this happened, the library's yew tree began to bleed wisps of blue. It was moving its lifeblood upwards, sending all its blue flame into Aeverum and Kala's Tynk. Seconds later, there was a flash of blinding blue light.

The yew tree was left dead, and in its place, there was a

luminous Tynk. The toy's core was now covered in sapphire light.

"No, give the fire back to the tree," Kala said. "Give it back!"

She rushed over to her Tynk and reached for it. But the Tynk propped itself onto its wheels and sped away. The toy moved without Kala's touch: it rotated in place and glowed with blue fire.

Kala reached her hand closer to the toy, and when she grazed its outer wheels, it leapt away from her again.

"Hey, come back!" Kala scrambled towards the toy, but it danced farther away from her. "Stop, just wait!"

Kala lunged as a beautiful voice rushed through the air. It was the sound of tiny metal hammers striking a steel shell, a mechanical music that turned into words.

"Excuse me." The voice was coming from inside the Tynk. No, it *was* the Tynk.

"What are you going to throw me off this tree?" the Tynk said. "You can't just kill me. I hardly know you!"

16

Kala tumbled down the side of the yew tree and fell sharply onto one of its lower branches. With aching ribs, she looked up at her Tynk. Kala thought she was imagining things. But no, her Tynk was still spinning freely.

"Was that... were you *talking?*" Kala sputtered.

"Maybe I was," the Tynk answered. Her voice was a beautiful chorus of metal. She wheeled herself about, rolling circles over the yew tree. "If I *was* speaking, what's it to you?"

"You're a Tynk," Kala replied. "Tynks don't talk."

"I'm just me," the Tynk answered. "And *me* can talk."

"Is there someone inside you?" Kala asked. "Someone who's making the voice?"

"My voice comes from me. I just told you that."

"Yeah, but what is *me?*" Kala eased her way back up the yew tree. She reached the same limb as her Tynk.

"Does that mean you know things?" Kala asked. "Are there ideas in your head… I mean your orb?"

"There are things I know and things I don't," the Tynk said matter-of-factly. "Why should I tell *you* about it?"

The Tynk slowed to a stop.

"Well, I can remember a voice," she said. "And then, I could feel something below me. Like the ground, but wrinkly."

"So you can feel stuff?" Kala asked.

"Do you mean touch? Or feelings?"

"I guess both?"

"Well then both! I think… Or maybe neither," the Tynk went on. "Why are you acting so strange? What's with all the questions?"

"Do you know what you are?" Kala asked. Gently, she ran a finger over one of the Tynk's wheels.

"You called me a Tynk, so that's what I am."

"Well, do you know what a Tynk is?"

The metal toy paused for a moment, then spun her wheels every which way. "I suppose I don't."

"You're a Tynk Two," Kala said. "Your wheels move in opposite directions, around this steel ball that you have. When everything's spinning, people like to look at you."

"Why would they do that?"

"They can't help it," Kala said. "It takes their minds off things."

"Do *you* look at Tynks?"

Kala felt a pang of guilt. She thought of the mother's warning about Tynks. A few feet away, she watched her own Tynk flip its wheels around.

"So this is all I do?" the toy asked.

"That's all *Tynks* do," Kala said. "But you're not just a Tynk… not anymore."

Kala moved towards the place where Aeverum once burned on the yew tree.

"There used to be a fire here," she said. "A *Kindler* fire. It held all the Imagination in the world. I think you have a big piece of it — the *last* piece of it — inside you."

"I have imaginary fire?"

"I think you *are* Imagination," Kala said. "At least, part of it. Someone took the rest. Can I see something?"

"It depends what *something* is."

Kala cracked open the Tynk by the thin seam in her inner orb. Inside, Kala found the same assortment of gears as before, only now, they were cloaked in blue fire. There was something else, too. The iron rotor that Kala made with her father was now stuck to the metal around it. Unmovable.

"That's weird," Kala said.

"What's weird? Am *I* weird?"

Opened, Kala could see how the Tynk created her voice. Like the thud of hammers on a piano's strings, the Tynk struck its gears against its spherical shell. Different sized cogs made different sounds. Together, they were a voice of music.

"Close me up," the Tynk said. "Your breath smells."

Kala saw these words forming in her fingers. "You can smell?" she asked.

"Would you shut me already? I don't like being *opened.*"

"Why not? You should see what's going on in here."

The Tynk fired her wheels against Kala's fingers. "Can we open you up, too? We'll start at your heart, then go to the vocal cords. It'll be wonderful!"

"Okay, point made," Kala said, twisting the Tynk shut.

"I'll be opened only when I allow it." The Tynk's voice wasn't quite as glorious now, muffled by its steel cover. "And I know what seeing and smelling are, to answer your question. But I can't do them."

"Then how do you stay on the tree? Shouldn't you just spin right off?"

"I have knowledge of everything, including this tree. I know every one of its branches, leaves and acorns."

"Really?"

"No."

The Tynk started spinning inside Kala's lap, then zipped along the tree that held them both, teetering along its edge but never spilling over.

"I can feel where things are and where they're not," the Tynk said. "Like where your big fire used to be."

"How do you do that?" Kala asked.

"Lots of things have their own fire, if that's what you want to call it. You do and so did this tree. They're not the same as the one that I have, but they're similar." The Tynk came to another stop. "That's how I know where things are and where they're not. You see with your eyes. I see with the fire."

Intrigued, Kala sat up onto her heels.

"What else can you feel?" she asked. "What about things that are far away? Other fires?"

"My sight isn't limited like yours. But the closer the fires are, the stronger they burn for me."

"Is there anything else like *your* fire?" Kala went on. "It might not be close, but it would feel the same. And it would be powerful… *really* powerful."

The Tynk paused for a moment. "Maybe," she said. "It's hard to tell."

"Can you take me? To anything you think is like your fire?"

"I can do that… But what are you going to do for me?"

"Do for you?" Kala asked. "What do Tynks want?"

"You said I was more than a Tynk."

"You are!" Kala said. "So what do you want then?"

The Tynk spun a few circles in front of Kala, thinking. "If I'm different, then I want to look different."

"You want a makeover?"

"Not a makeover. More like an upgrade."

Kala looked around the library for something that might suit her Tynk. There was a heap of wood, leather and paper on the ground; nothing worthy of an *upgrade*. So, looking above, Kala found a dead leaf and rolled it through her hands. Then, Kala tucked it into the seam that ran through her Tynk.

"There," she said. "A crown... a crown for the queen of all Tynks!"

The steel toy flit about with her new decoration, crinkling the leaf as it went. After a minute's worth of testing, the Tynk adjusted the leaf so that her wheels wouldn't crush it.

"This will do," the Tynk said. "Now keep up."

"Keep up?"

The Tynk sped away. She bounced down the yew tree's limbs, reached the floor and continued rolling away. Picking up speed, the Tynk hurtled into the library's doors — just hard enough to crack them open — and disappeared down the road to TynkerVille.

17

Kala watched in horror as her Tynk raced down the road. Bouncing on her outer wheels, the Tynk zipped beneath caravans and whistled around strangers. Kala sprinted to keep up with her metal toy, praying it wouldn't be crushed by a passing cart.

"Excuse me. Sorry!"

Kala dashed between horses and drew the eyes of countless travelers, and by the time she caught up with her Tynk, she was well down the road into the heart of Holloton. She looked rather ridiculous; wide-eyed, with blood still gushing from her forehead. But Kala didn't care. She had a magic Tynk cupped in her palms and that was all that mattered.

"You can't just roll away like that," Kala said. "And no

talking, either!"

"No one tells me what to do. Only *I* tell *me* what to do," the Tynk huffed.

"Look, there aren't any other Tynks like you. If someone sees you — sees *us* — we're both done for. I'll be locked up and you'll be pulled apart piece by piece!"

"Fine… I can be quiet," the Tynk said. "As long as you don't tell me what to do."

"Fine."

For the first time in many minutes, Kala looked up from the road and her Tynk. Holloton's gargantuan center was growing closer.

"So what do I call you?" Kala asked.

"Whatever you'd like," her Tynk answered.

"So you want to be *Tynk*, just like the rest of them?"

"I have nothing to do with them. I was made in your fire, not in some factory."

"You *were* made in a factory. Just not the whole stolen-blue-flame part."

"I was not made in a factory," the Tynk declared. "And that is that."

Kala smirked at the metal in her hands. "I never knew Aeverum had such an attitude."

"Who's that?"

"Aeverum? That's the blue fire you took."

"I like that," the Tynk said. Her metal innards thumped a little harder. "That name, *Iverum*, I'd like to take it."

"You can't just take it."

"Why not? I'm sure there are hundreds of people named... what's your name?"

"Kala. And I've never met another person with my name. But that's not the point."

"Then what is the point?"

Kala stopped walking and scratched at her nose. "Aeverum's not like other names," she said. "No one would know who you're talking about. You or the fire? The fire or you? Unless you're saying that both of you are the same?"

"We most definitely are not the same. I am me and no one else is."

"Then you deserve a special name," Kala said, walking again. "One that no one else has. What if we made Aeverum shorter?"

"I already made it smaller."

"No, not the actual fire," Kala said. "Just its name. We need something close to Aeverum, but different."

"Like what?"

"I don't know. Maybe Rumi? Or how about Remi?"

"No. Those don't fit right."

Kala sighed. Holloton's skyscrapers now teemed above her, roaring with torches and people so high they could hardly be seen. Speaking to her Tynk, Kala hardly noticed as her small neighborhood slipped away in favor of the wooden towers.

Beneath these structures, there were strings of strange shops lining the road. One sold furniture made from iron. Another sold lubricant for old Tynks. *Our Spins Last Hours*, the shop's window said.

All the shops' windows were etched with the flowing *T's*.

They were all owned by TynkerVille.

"Welcome home," Kala whispered to her Tynk.

The ground grew soft beneath her feet as she stepped further down the road. Kala saw a young girl slosh a bucket of water onto a pile of filthy clothes. There was a boy flicking beads of sweat as he ran from a furious storekeeper. The boy passed an older man, who leaned forward and hacked a ball of phlegm onto the ground. Wincing, Kala let her heel squish deeper into the dirt.

"You're lucky you can't see," she said to her Tynk.

"I already told you I can see, don't be so small-minded."

"How many fingers am I holding up then?" Kala asked, lifting three of her fingers.

"Three," the toy said immediately.

"How can you know that?"

"Because I have a big mind and I guessed with it," the Tynk said. "…and because you changed the air when you lifted your hand. The air gets tighter when things take its space."

"The air gets tighter?" Kala asked.

"That's what I said," her Tynk answered. "There's a lot happening here, I can feel it. Above and below the ground."

Kala looked to the side of the road. She found a storm grate collecting a stream of green water.

"What's below us?" Kala asked. She never thought anything

could exist below TynkerVille's buildings.

"The hand not the fingers, remember? There's something big down there, but I can't see what it is."

As Kala's Tynk spoke, its shell grew warm. "Forget the sewers," the Tynk said. Her voice changed; it grew hollow and monotone.

But Kala didn't notice this change. She was staring blankly at the storm grate and the dying plants that wound through its bars.

"What about Ivy?" Kala asked.

"What about it?" her Tynk said. Her normal voice returned, full of metal and music.

"You still need a name," Kala went on. "Ivy comes from the middle of Aeverum."

"I'm not a poisonous plant."

"No one's going to think that. How about Evie, then?"

At this, the Tynk's outer rings began glowing in blue.

"Evie... we can try that," the Tynk said. "Just for now."

"Just for now," Kala echoed.

And with Evie fixed warmly between her hands, Kala stepped towards the center of Holloton, towards TynkerVille. She heard water rushing below her, deep into unseen places beneath the ground.

Kala thought she could hear something ticking, too. She stopped to bring her ear closer to the gutter, but its smell was too foul and she lurched away.

Kala walked deeper into TynkerVille instead, towards its

lights and its sound and she hoped, her parents. Candles warmed the back of Kala's neck. The ground squished with each of her steps.

18

As Kala moved deeper into TynkerVille, she wondered where her parents might be. She looked up and saw impossibly tall buildings, each with hundreds of tiny rooms. Below these were dozens of shops, all mazes of goods and customers. Kala's parents could be anywhere, she only hoped they were being held together.

But at least Kala had her priorities straight. Unable to find the fire coursing through her limbs, Kala knew she needed to find her mother before anything else.

Then, Kala needed to find the rest of Aeverum. If the Kindler and her blue fire weren't reunited, the world's supply of Imagination would wither away.

"Are we almost there, Evie?" Kala asked.

"Shush, I'm focusing," the Tynk answered. She led Kala deep into the heart of Holloton. They avoided the slender alleys where the drained — the ones with no Imagination — were lined against the walls.

"It's different here," Evie said. "Something's changing."

Glancing around, Kala agreed. Holloton's crowds had dwindled, and no one could be seen in the windows above. Kala felt a lump rise into her throat. She followed Evie's directions for a few more blocks before they came to a stop.

"What is *that?*" Kala gasped.

Evie had brought her to a massive, silver fence. It was an impenetrable wall that guarded something magnificent.

"This is it," Evie said. "Your fire's in there."

"Mom," Kala breathed.

"Your mother's a fire?"

"She has it inside her," Kala said. "Her own fire is even bigger than Aeverum, but she needs all of it to stay alive."

Kala wrapped her palms around the fence and stared at a building that sat a hundred yards away. It was a structure unlike anything Kala had ever seen, made of pure metal. The building reached five stories into the air in gorgeous, flowing curves.

Its spires all pointed to the center of the building, where a slender tower rose high above the earth. The top of the tower glimmered with three massive stones: one was the color of a ruby, another beamed like an emerald and the third looked like a sapphire. And, after studying these stones for a moment,

Kala wondered if they were *actual* jewels.

"How do we get inside the fence?" Kala asked. She wrapped her fist a little tighter around the silver bar and tried to find an entrance to the metal building. But Kala saw no windows, doors, or gates along the fence. There was only a string of letters — *TynkerVille*.

"So this is it," Kala said. "TynkerVille's actual Factory. This is where they made you, Evie."

But there were no chimneys on the roof of this building. There was no smoke pumping into the air or signs of anything being produced. Kala scratched at her head.

"It doesn't make any sense. If Mom was the enemy, why would they bring her *inside* TynkerVille?" Kala wondered. "First Mom gets stolen, then my Tynk starts talking… why did *you* bring me here, Evie?"

"I was following the fire like you asked me to," Evie answered. "You can put me down now."

"What if they swapped you… swapped you with *my* Tynk?" Kala said. "They could have done it when I was knocked out."

Kala started pacing.

"My parents get taken by TynkerVille and I've been following their Tynk right up to their gate. This is what they wanted the whole time!"

"I don't work for anyone," Evie said. "I was *just* following the fire."

"How can I know that?"

"You can't and I don't have to explain myself!"

Evie fired her wheels and freed herself from Kala's hands. She dropped to the ground and rolled away.

"Go ahead, leave!" Kala shouted. "You got me here. That's what they wanted, right?"

Kala watched her Tynk vanish around the street. But, a moment later, she felt her rage start to fade. She wondered if Evie was right. Kala thought she could feel her mother somewhere inside TynkerVille.

Kala started running the length of the building's silver fence. Every now and again, she threw her hands against it and pulled. When that didn't work, she tried squeezing between the small gaps in the fence's silver bars.

"Let. Me. In!" Kala screamed. "Mom, can you hear me? Are you in there?"

But none of it worked. After a half hour, Kala stumbled to the ground and sank into the wet dirt. She could still feel her mother just a hundred yards away. But there was no way of getting into TynkerVille.

"You lost everyone," Kala said, sinking deeper into the ground. "You couldn't even keep a Tynk."

Kala started crying. She wept until her chest hurt... until noise broke everywhere her. Kala threw her hands against her ears, but this does little to stop the new sound.

It was a familiar noise made of words that seemed to leap right out of the air. They were stringing themselves into sentences... merging together... becoming an announcement.

<u>19</u>

"Can we, the representatives of TynkerVille, have your undivided attention?"

A voice crashed through the air.

"It's time to announce the winners of our first Tour of TynkerVille!"

Dozens of heads popped out from the skyscrapers above. But Kala was looking elsewhere. She saw something familiar rolling around a nearby street corner: Evie.

"Hot, hot!!!" the Tynk said, bouncing into Kala's leg. "My shell, it's burning!"

Even through her clothes, Kala could feel Evie's orb. The steel was scalding.

"What's happening?" Kala shouted. "Roll in the mud!"

At once, the Tynk rolled into a filthy puddle and used it to cool down. The ground simmered beneath Evie's rolling, and soon, her shell grew cool.

"What was that all about?" Kala asked.

"I don't know," Evie said. "It's like my gears turn to lava."

"Weird," Kala sighed. "Look, about before… I'm sorry, Evie. I shouldn't have—"

"Four members of our public, selected at random, will spend a day inside TynkerVille," the everywhere voice cut in, drowning out Kala. *"They will work side by side with our Designer."*

This made Kala's heart thump.

The winner gets inside TynkerVille, she thought to herself.

"Our first participant is Harrison Druthers!" TynkerVille's voice said.

Behind these words, Kala heard noise coming from a distance. A crowd was closing in on TynkerVille.

"… Second will be Gwen Duckworth!"

Kala went rigid at this name.

"I know her," she whispered. "Gwen was in the library a few days ago."

"Has she seen my fire?" Evie asked.

"Maybe, but most people think Aeverum is just a blue candle."

"A candle! I'll have you know I was not born—"

"Our third participant is Finbar Frampington!"

The hope Kala felt moments ago was quickly replaced with worry. Three names had been called and none of them were

Kala Blaise. Her chances of getting inside TynkerVille were slipping away.

People began pouring into the streets. They circled TynkerVille and wrapped their hands around its silver fence. Some looked at their Tynks. Others stared at the gorgeous metal building that birthed the toys.

Kala backed away from them all and stepped onto a crate at the foot of a wooden skyscraper. There, she pulled Evie to her chest and watched. All the people around her had new Tynks. That meant they were all entered in TynkerVille's lottery. The odds weren't looking good.

"One more name," Kala whispered. She imagined two words breaking through the air, *Kala Blaise,* and tried wishing them into existence.

"Our final participant..." the voice of TynkerVille said, *"...will be Marley Mayfair!"*

Kala collapsed into a heap. She was just as far from her mother as when she started.

"All who have been chosen have three hours to claim their spot. Good day."

With that, TynkerVille's voice went silent.

All around Kala, a stampede marched on TynkerVille's fence. They wanted to catch a glimpse of the metal building, and the thin seam of light that was now emerging from it. The beam came from a pair of slender doors that were slowly opening.

The crowds gasped as a man emerged from TynkerVille.

Kala clambered higher up the wooden skyscraper to get a glimpse of him. She gasped.

"You're the Designer!?" Kala cried.

The man from TynkerVille wore a flowing, grey cloak and had metal veins racing up his neck. His eyes were stuck in a blank, grey stare. He was the same man from the Holloton Library, the one who stole Aeverum and Luana Blaise.

The metal man walked alone and drew the awe of everyone in the crowd. Everyone except for Kala, who felt rage boil in her bones. She wanted to kill the metal man, break into his castle and reunite her mother with Aeverum.

But Kala knew that couldn't happen. TynkerVille's fence was impenetrable, and even if Kala made it through, she'd stand little chance of passing the Designer. Kala remembered the sick power that came from his arms and legs.

The crowds around Kala didn't share this fear. They climbed TynkerVille's fence and some of them even reached the silver barbed wire that curled around its top.

But as more people rose, a deep trembling came from underground. It sent TynkerVille's silver fence upward; foot by foot, the enclosure rose high into the air until it was double its original height.

"He's the one who stole my mother," Kala said to Evie, lifting the toy towards the Designer. "He could jump across the whole library in one leap. I've never seen anything like it."

"There's barely any fire in him," Evie said. "Must have strong legs?"

"More than that," Kala said. "He has metal all inside him. I don't know how it got there."

Her eyes were drawn to movement in the crowd. People were shuffling around a screaming, old man.

"I'm Harry Druthers, let me by you dolts!" this man shouted. "Didn't you hear? It's me, Harry Druthers!"

When this man finally reached TynkerVille's fence, a hideous crack sounded. Two silver rods disappeared into the ground, allowed the old man to pass, then immediately shot back into the air. All eyes were now on Harrison Druthers. He was an ancient man with wild hair and an even wilder smile.

Stretching onto her toes, Kala watched the Designer nod at Harrison, then wave a hand towards TynkerVille's beam of light. Harrison walked straight into the metal castle. It was that easy.

"Kala, what about the Duckworth girl?" Evie growled. "What does she look like?"

"Why do you keep doing that?" Kala asked.

"Doing what?"

"Your voice changed again. It happened by the sewer, too."

"It sounds the same to me... I asked what Gwen looks like."

"What does that have to do with anything?"

"Does she look like you?" Evie asked.

Kala rubbed her head. "Maybe. We have similar hair, but hers is a little shorter."

"You can be her," Evie said. "That's how we get you into TynkerVille."

"That would never work," Kala said, shaking her head. "What happens when Gwen shows up and I'm already inside?"

"You make sure she *doesn't* show up."

"You mean kill her?"

"No!" Evie said. "I mean give her money or just tell her you *really* need to get into TynkerVille!"

"I know where Gwen lives. Or at least, where she used to," Kala went on. "Before this was all TynkerVille, me and Mom used to go around raising money for the library. I'm not sure I can find her house anymore, though. A lot's changed."

"You've got three hours to figure it out," Evie said. "You can find *anything* in three hours."

"It won't work," Kala sighed.

"Do you have a better idea?"

Kala stared at her Tynk, and realized Evie was right. This was her best, maybe *only*, chance at getting into TynkerVille.

And so, after a deep breath, Kala walked away from TynkerVille's crowds. She came to a stop a few blocks later.

"What's happening?" Evie asked.

"Can I open you one more time?" Kala said.

"For what?"

"I have to check something; it'll only take a minute. It's important, Evie."

Kala twisted open Evie's orb. Inside the Tynk, there was a maze of gears and a whisking blue flame. There was also the iron rotor that Kala made with her father.

109

"I should have believed you," Kala said, twisting Evie shut. "No one replaced you. You were my Tynk the whole time."

20

"All the streets should still work the same," Kala said. Behind her, Evie rolled to keep up. "Holloton is still a big grid. Even if they added all these skyscrapers."

Holloton's outer roads were empty, and it took Kala just a few minutes to wind her way through her old memories. After jogging fourteen blocks north and three to the east, she found the Duckworth's home. It was covered in black grime and trembled beneath a skyscraper that had been built right on top of it.

From the road, Kala peered through the home's windows. She saw Gwen Duckworth zipping around her kitchen, leaping from chairs to tables to cabinets then back again.

"I did it!" Gwen squealed. "TynkerVille wants *me!*"

"You didn't do anything," Kala muttered.

Upstairs, Gwen's twin sister stormed into their bedroom. She chucked pillows at the wall, then collapsed onto her bed and screamed. After a minute of shouting, Melissa opened a tall cabinet. She plucked her sister's clothes from their hangers and dragged them across the floor until they were covered with dust.

"Melissa's been coming to the library for years," Kala whispered. "She always had a thing for dirt."

"That's a weird thing to have a thing for," Evie muttered.

"Not everyone has a thing," Kala shrugged. "At least she's got a thing."

Melissa kept going until every last piece of her sister's clothing was filthy. Satisfied, she laid back in bed and smiled. Her sister Gwen was still zooming around the kitchen below, and for the first time, Kala noticed the twins' parents. They both seemed totally unconcerned with Gwen's admission to the Tour of TynkerVille. After a moment, Kala realized why.

The Duckworth parents had Tynks of their own whirring in their palms. Every now and then, they would look up to see Gwen swinging from a light or leaping from a coffee stand. They waved their fists and mumbled at her, but eventually, they returned to the spin of their Tynks.

"What if we lock Gwen in a cabinet or something? I don't think her parents would notice."

"Her twin would find her."

"Right," Kala sighed. She tapped her foot in thought. "What

if I gave her *you*, Evie? Not forever, but just long enough to keep her distracted. There's no way Gwen would ever leave a talking Tynk!"

"I'm not some chess piece for you to play with," Evie said. "Absolutely not. Out of the question."

Inside the Duckworth's home, Gwen began stuffing a bag full of her things. She moved upstairs and threw in a filthy shirt as her sister snickered away in bed.

"She's getting ready to leave," Kala said. "We have to get in there. Look, just don't talk while we're inside. They can't know you're not a normal Tynk."

"I'll talk when I choose to and be quiet when I choose to."

"Then I suggest you *choose* to be quiet right now!"

Kala waited until Gwen moved back downstairs, then sprinted to the side of the Duckworth's house and began climbing.

"What's going on out there?" Evie asked from Kala's pocket. "We're going up and I don't like heights!"

"You were born in a tree," Kala said.

"Does every acorn like dangling from its branch?"

"If you didn't kill our yew tree, I could have asked them."

Kala's voice carried farther than she expected. It drew Melissa Duckworth up from bed and over to her bedroom window.

"Library girl!" Melissa shouted, staring down at Kala. "What are you doing here? Why are you climbing?"

"Look, I don't have a lot of time — *hey!*"

Melissa waved a hand at Kala and tried to nudge her off the window.

"Don't just *push* me," Kala said.

"If someone's snooping in your window you're allowed to push them," Melissa said. "It's one of those unworded rules."

"Unwritten," Kala muttered, dodging another shove. "Would you just listen for a minute?"

Melissa tucked her hands at her sides.

"Thank you," Kala said. "I have an offer to make."

"What is it?"

"Your sister... We're going to take away what Gwen wants more than anything else. She'll be miserable."

Melissa stepped back from her window. "I'm listening."

"Can I come in?" Kala tried lifting her foot onto the window but Melissa stopped her.

"Window lurkers don't get to come right in," she said. "Give me more."

Kala readjusted her position on the side of the home. She was surprised to find Evie quiet. For once, she seemed to be cooperating.

"As I'm sure you heard," Kala started, "your sister was chosen for the Tour of TynkerVille. In three—"

"What is it exactly?" Melissa asked. "A game?"

"It's a tour. TynkerVille chose four people and they each have three hours to—"

"What's the prize?"

"Would you let me talk?"

Melissa stared straight at Kala. "You're the one hanging out the window. Don't forget it."

"The winner gets a new Tynk," Kala huffed, and when Melissa didn't interrupt her, she continued. "I need to get inside TynkerVille. I don't care if I win, there's just something I need in there. But the more important thing is your sister. I want to take Gwen's place in the Tour. I need to be her, for just a day. Can you help me with that?"

Melissa walked a few circles around the foot of her bed. "So Gwen will be miserable?"

"She won't talk for weeks," Kala said.

A smile came over Melissa. She walked back to her window and stuck out her hand.

"Then you better come in, library girl."

<u>21</u>

Kala pulled herself into the Duckworth's home and reminded herself that time was not on her side. She had three hours to make it inside TynkerVille.

"So what's the plan?" Melissa asked.

"We need to make one," Kala said. "You know your sister better than anyone else. How do we keep her from leaving?"

Melissa looked down at her feet. "I'm only saying this once," she muttered. "But Gwen's stronger than me. I can't stop her... not with my hands, at least."

"That's fine," Kala said. "What does she like to do? Is there somewhere she'd rather be than TynkerVille?"

"Gwen loves dirt. Oh, and finding worms underneath tree bark."

"Okay… what does she like to eat?"

"You know, the usual stuff."

Melissa shrugged, and Kala was starting to realize she was pretty useless. But, after taking a quick glance around the Duckworth's bedroom, Kala thought she had an idea of her own.

She whisked through the room and started opening drawers. Kala found a bunch of disgusting things: a jar full of dead bugs; dolls with their eyes plucked out; a half-loaf of bread that was green with mold. And as Kala continued her search, Melissa rushed over and tackled her.

"I'm just looking for your Tynk," Kala gasped. "I'm not your sister, you can't just wrestle me!"

"I'm stopping an attempted robbery!" Melissa shouted.

With a burst of strength, Melissa pulled Kala from the cupboard and they both went tumbling backwards. Evie fell from Kala's pocket and rolled to a stop against the room's far wall. Below, a pair of footsteps began rising upstairs.

"We have to make Gwen look at a Tynk," Kala whispered to Melissa. "You hold her down and I'll hold the Tynk up to her eyes."

"Fine," Melissa scowled. She reached into her pocket and rolled her own Tynk over to Kala.

Kala grabbed the lifeless toy and noticed how close it looked to Evie from afar. But up close, it was clear that Melissa's Tynk was missing something vital. It had no blue fire streaming through its gears, no voice of music stirring in its core.

"Hey dirt breath, I heard something up here." Gwen Duckworth bounced into her bedroom. Her eyes immediately fell onto Kala. "Library girl!"

Next, a mad howling erupted. Melissa Duckworth flew out from behind her bedroom door and leapt onto her sister's shoulders. Kala watched the twins struggle, then ran towards Gwen and held the lifeless Tynk just beneath her eyes.

"Hold her still!" Kala shouted.

The plan didn't work. Gwen didn't fall into the spin of the Tynk, and with a strong shake, threw her sister right off her back.

Kala was left scrambling around the twins' bedroom in search of another idea. She found more gross things — balls of hair, ants marching through cracks in the floor — but nothing of any use.

But then Kala saw Evie sitting quietly against the wall.

"Start spinning!" Kala shouted. "Spin now, Evie!"

"Are you sure?" Evie asked.

"Just do it!"

Evie set in motion, spinning gloriously and becoming a typhoon of steel and blue light. Kala picked up Evie, rushed towards the Duckworth twins and held up her Tynk. This time, Gwen's eyes were captured.

"What is… Where did you…"

Gwen mumbled uselessly. Evie was too magnificent to look away from, as beautiful as metal and fire could be. Noise was swept from the bedroom and all that could be heard was the whine of Evie's perfect gears.

Kala walked backwards and, like fish bound to a hook, Gwen followed with her sister in tow.

Next, Kala reached up with her free hand. She noticed the thick, glass orb that illuminated the bedroom, very much like the one in her father's workshop. Kala grabbed this orb, and with the Duckworth girls still mesmerized, dropped Evie inside.

Evie jittered around the glass bowl and quickly gained her balance. Her spins were magnified by the glass and the eyes of the Duckworth twins were struck wide.

But soon, a change came over Gwen and Melissa. A green haze started pouring from their eyes. Gasping, Kala tried to pull the glass orb and Evie away. But something stopped her as she remembered that this was her only ticket into TynkerVille… her only chance of finding her parents.

More smoke poured from Melissa and Gwen. It was Imagination streaming out from their eyes. This went on for a full minute, until Melissa and Gwen dropped to the ground with smoky grey eyes.

"Are you still in there?" Kala whispered.

She waved her arm in front of the twins, but they didn't stir. They'd become just like the strangers who lined the dark alleys around their home.

"Come on, wake up!"

Kala slapped Melissa's knee, then pinched Gwen's foot. But still, there was nothing from the girls. Kala began to feel nauseous and moved towards the window.

"It's not forever," she whispered to herself. "Their fires will come back."

"What did you do to them?" Evie asked. "I can't feel them anymore."

Kala didn't answer.

"Does that mean they're distracted? Is the plan going to work?"

Kala climbed back out the window with Evie in tow, and took one last look at Melissa and Gwen before stepping down to the road. She saw two sets of grey eyes and two blank faces.

"It's not forever," Kala whispered.

"What are you talking about?" Evie asked.

"I'll find Mom and Aeverum. She'll make them more fire."

22

During the walk back to TynkerVille, Kala couldn't stop thinking of the Duckworth girls. Their eyes were so grey… their faces were so empty…

"So why do you think that Designer guy took your mother?" Evie asked.

Kala was stirred from her thoughts. She realized how easy moving through Holloton's streets had become. The roads were totally empty now, because everyone in Holloton was gathered outside TynkerVille's fence.

"They took my father first. We think he's the one making all the Tynks," Kala said to Evie. "And my mother is the Kindler. She's supposed to build the fire you were made in."

"I guess TynkerVille doesn't like your family all that much,"

Evie sighed. "So they have your mother *and* her fire?"

"Yep, I'm sure that's what you felt inside their fence," Kala said. "They probably want to let Aeverum burn out and keep my mother from building it back up."

"What happens then?"

"Nothing good," Kala sighed. "Remember how you couldn't feel Gwen and Melissa after you spun in front of them?"

"I could sense them at first," Evie said. "But then there was nothing. They vanished."

"If TynkerVille gets their way, that's going to happen to everyone," Kala sighed. "That's why I have to find my mother before anything else. She's the only one that can keep Aeverum from going out."

"Can't you do that?" Evie asked. "Didn't your mother ever teach you?"

"I'm not like her," Kala said. She flexed her flameless hands.

There was a new taste in the air, sweat and metal mixing together. Kala and Evie were getting close to TynkerVille. They could hear the crowds collected outside the factory's silver fence.

"Remember, you're not Kala anymore," Evie said. "You have to *be* Gwen Duckworth if this is ever going to work."

"Right," Kala answered.

"Didn't you say Gwen's hair is shorter than yours? Shouldn't you cut yours?"

"I'll be fine."

"Kala, you're not just strolling into some bookstore. You're trying to get into TynkerVille!"

The force in Evie's words drew Kala from her daze. She had fallen back into her own thoughts. A stolen Kindler... A missing father... Twins with four grey eyes...

Now, Kala could smell the putrid air around her. She thought of the metal man, the Designer, standing guard outside his castle.

"What should I do with my hair?" Kala asked. Her hands trembled as she imagined walking up to the Designer. "I was wrong, Evie. I look nothing like Gwen!"

"Stop it, your heart's going to burst through your mouth," Evie said. "Use one of my gears, it should be sharp enough. Go ahead, open me up."

Kala found Evie's seam and pried it open. One of her gears was sticking out, a fine rotor made of copper.

"Take it," Evie said. "I'll put it back in place when you're done. Just be quick."

Kala plucked the rotor away and sliced away a few locks of her hair. Once she was done, Kala tried to put Evie's gear back in place.

But a change had come over the Tynk: a small spout of blue fire was leaking from Evie's core. It only stopped when Kala shoved the copper rotor back in place.

"Evie, you hurt yourself!" Kala said.

"I'm fine, don't worry about it."

"Why would you do that?"

"I didn't know it would happen!" Evie cried. "How about a thank you? You're not so good at those, you know."

Kala studied the insides of her Tynk. Evie appeared to be back in order; her gears were thumping away just like before.

"Do you feel more like a Duckworth now?" Evie asked.

Kala ran a hand through her hair and felt a sharp prickle. "I feel like me, but with a bad haircut."

"Well, that's something," Evie said.

Kala and Evie reached the crowds that were clawing towards TynkerVille's fence. Kala rushed up to the back of the mass and tried to find a way through. But every gap she found quickly closed.

"Hey, let me in!" Kala shouted. "I'm Gwen Duckworth!"

Kala's voice was one of hundreds. No one moved out of her way and she made no progress towards TynkerVille. Kala thought of the old man, Harrison Druthers, and how the crowds had bent around his voice. Why weren't they doing the same for her?

"Gwen Duckworth!" Kala shouted. "I'm Gwen Duckworth! Make room, Gwen Duckworth is coming through!"

Kala marched forward and slammed right into the back of an old woman. She fell to the ground, breathless, and searched for another way through. She thought first of the sewers. Maybe Kala could travel *underneath* the crowds and pop back onto the road right in front of TynkerVille!

Kala jogged over to the nearest sewer grate and tried peering through its bars. She immediately leapt back and wheezed. The air coming from the sewers was thick and harsh. Kala doubted she could breathe below ground, much less find her way into TynkerVille.

Kala looked to her last hope: the sky. She saw hundreds of empty apartments and their mighty skyscrapers teetering in the wind. Everyone had left their homes to gather around TynkerVille's fence. There were no faces in the windows above.

But as Kala searched the wooden skyscrapers, her eye caught a flicker of movement. It came from a boy who was rushing behind a window six stories above.

TynkerVille had called him Finbar Frampington, but Kala knew him by a different name.

Fin. Just Fin.

23

Kala started counting windows. First, the ones that ran upward. Then, the ones that ran from left to right. She found Fin's exact location in the wooden skyscraper, then rushed inside.

This was Kala's first time inside one of Holloton's new, mighty buildings. She found herself in a lobby whose floor was stacked two-feet-high with trash. Dashing through the horrific smell, Kala started up a huge, spiral stairway. It was made from rotting wood and wound all the way to the top of the skyscraper.

"Six floors up," Kala said to herself, pinching her nose. "Five over."

Kala's feet creaked with every step she took. She thought of using the stairway's guardrail but decided against it when she noticed the mysterious brown liquid dripping from it. No one passed Kala as she moved upward. Everyone was still gathered outside TynkerVille's fence.

"Where are we going?" Evie asked from Kala's pocket.

"We're meeting a friend," Kala answered. "He helped me buy you."

"Oh, I like him already!"

When she reached the sixth floor, Kala found a hallway full of unlocked apartments. There were clothes scattered everywhere, and when Kala moved five doors down the hallway, she found out why. Fin was sitting cross-legged on the ground making a giant rope out of shirts, shorts, socks and anything else he could find.

"You better not use my coat for that," Kala said.

Fin jumped with surprise and held out his walking stick like a sword. But when he realized it was Kala, he lowered his stick and sighed.

"You?" Fin said. "How'd you find me?"

Kala thought of telling Fin about her plan to enter TynkerVille but decided against it.

"I came to see what all the noise was about," Kala said. "Then I looked up and saw you. What's the rope for?"

"My name got called, didn't you hear?" Fin said.

"Yeah, Finbar Frampington."

"Don't use that name. I don't like it."

"You never answered my question. What's the rope for?"

Fin looked down from the sixth story window onto TynkerVille's crowds.

"They wouldn't let me through," he said. "So I'm finding my own way into TynkerVille."

"You're going to climb the fence?" Kala asked. "It can raise itself, you know."

"Something like that," Fin said. He looked up from his rope. "I have to get in there, Kala. Can you help me?"

"I thought you don't like Tynks?" Kala said. "They're an investment, remember?"

"I've got my own reasons," Fin answered.

He handed Kala one end of his rope and tied something metal onto the other side. It was a Tynk that had been turned inside out. Dozens of sharp gears stuck out from its shell.

"You'll need you to hold onto that," Fin said to Kala. He started whirling the other end of rope overhead, then let it go.

It sailed out the window Tynk-first, flew right over TynkerVille's fence, and sunk into wet dirt. Fin tugged on his invention to make sure it was secure. He'd created a line of rope that reached from a sixth story window down onto the ground beyond TynkerVille's fence.

"You're going to climb down that?" Kala asked.

"Not quite." Fin said. He pulled off his coat, the one that used to be Kala's, and hung it over the top of the rope. "Hold on tight, Kala."

"Wait, you can't use my coat—*hey!*"

Kala fell forward as the rope in her hands got eighty pounds heavier. Fin leapt straight out the window and used his new coat to glide down his rope. Fin bumped over knots as he went but sailed over TynkerVille's fence with ease. He landed on the other side and waved up to Kala.

"Unbelievable," Kala muttered. "I bet he ruined my coat."

"Where'd he go?" Evie asked. "I liked him."

"He jumped out the window!"

"Why would he do that?"

Kala didn't answer. She took hold of Fin's rope and looked out the window. The height was staggering: six stories might as well have been a hundred.

"Kala, we're not following him right?" Evie asked. "You know I hate heights."

"Just keep quiet a minute," Kala said. She moved into the hallway and pulled on the guardrail. It wobbled from side to side but seemed to be holding.

"You'll have to do," Kala whispered.

"What'll have to do?" Evie cried. "I'm not jumping anywhere!"

Without speaking, Kala tied Fin's rope around the guardrail. She plucked a sweater off the ground and moved towards the window.

"Kala, I don't like this!"

Kala tucked Evie deep into her pocket and climbed out the window. She sat on the edge of its sill and wrapped her sweater over the top of Fin's rope. Kala felt her heart crash against her ribs. She refused to look at the drop below.

"Mom and Dad need you," Kala whispered. Then, she fell forward and screamed…

Kala flew down Fin's rope, secured by an old sweater and a moldy guardrail. The ride was pure chaos, but after a moment, Kala started to enjoy it. She was flying, just like the characters from her mother's stories.

But a moment later, the guardrail holding Kala and Evie snapped in two. They dropped suddenly, and only cleared TynkerVille's fence by a few inches. Gaining speed, they crashed into the ground and sank into TynkerVille's wet dirt.

"Evie, are you okay?" Kala asked. "Did I crush you?"

Kala scrambled to her feet and found Evie wallowing in a puddle of mud.

"Don't touch me," Evie said, rolling out from the dirt. "And don't *think* of talking to me."

But Kala threw her hands over Evie and hid her from Fin.

"What are you thinking?" Fin seethed. "You're crazy, Kala. Get back over the fence!"

"I need to get inside TynkerVille," Kala said. "I've got my reasons, just like you."

"You'll never get in," Fin laughed. "They didn't call your name. Fin, Harrison, Gwen, Marley… No Kala!"

"Gwen gave me her spot."

"No way."

"She did! And you're not going to tell anyone about it."

"So I'll just keep quiet while there's an *imposter* inside TynkerVille?" Fin huffed.

"That's right."

"And why would I do that?"

"Because I held the rope for you," Kala answered. "That means you owe me one."

"I helped you buy a Tynk."

"And you got my coat for that."

Fin froze. He looked Kala up and down, unsure what to make of her.

"Fine, I won't tell anyone," he said. "But don't get in my way when we're inside."

"Oh, and you'll have to call me Gwen. I don't want anyone to know my real name."

"Fine!"

Fin stomped away towards the Designer. The metal man hadn't budged an inch as Kala and Fin flew over his silver fence. He was still and mute.

The same could not be said for TynkerVille's crowds. They were absolutely furious that two children had made it over the fence and *not* them. They heaved trash and hunks of wood, then tried breaking down TynkerVille's mighty fence. But this failed. The silver was far too strong to be broken.

Kala looked ahead and saw Fin speaking with the Designer. The metal man stood at least three feet taller than the boy, but after a brief chat, he swept aside and let Fin pass.

Fin walked into TynkerVille, and just like Harrison Druthers, was swallowed by the building's blue light.

"My turn," Kala whispered.

Her legs quaked as she walked towards the Designer. She studied the metal veins running up his neck and remembered the larger skeleton that lay beneath his grey cloak. Luana's fiery whip had bounced right off it.

Would Kala's disguise really work against such a powerful man?

Would the Designer *really* believe that she was Gwen Duckworth?

The Designer was close now, just twenty yards away. For the first time, Kala got a good look at his face. The Designer was a somber looking man with milky-grey eyes. He stared blankly ahead, only shifting his gaze when Kala stumbled right up to him.

"Name?" the Designer said.

Sapphire sparks glimmered in his eyes as he spoke, but every time they did, a cloud of grey overwhelmed them. Kala was reminded of the Duckworth girls and their empty pupils. The Designer wasn't drained, though. So what was wrong with his eyes?

"Name?" the Designer repeated.

"Umm, Gwen," Kala mumbled. "My name's Gwen Duckworth."

The Designer seemed to come to life. His eyes flashed with blue and he smiled knowingly. Did he already know Kala's secret?

The Designer lifted his arm and chuckled. But as his fist rose, his eyes went grey and pain rushed through him.

It was just like the spasm Kala watched him endure in the library. The Designer's face twisted with anguish and revealed metal orbs inside each of his ears. This pain was brief, and when the Designer regained his composure, he held out his hand.

"Fine," he wheezed. "Run inside, *Gwen*."

Kala didn't wait. She ran from the Designer, more confused than ever, and pulled Evie from her pocket as TynkerVille's blue light swallowed them both.

"Evie, I think he's letting us in," Kala whispered. "Can you still feel my mother's fire? Are we getting closer?"

But something inside the Tynk was thumping madly.

"Quiet," Evie sputtered. "I need quiet."

"Are you hurt?" Kala said. "Did I fall on you?"

Evie said nothing more. Her shell was crackling with heat, just like it had twice before on their way to TynkerVille.

"What's happening to you?" Kala whispered. "Did I break you?"

Kala stepped deeper into TynkerVille's light and felt it brighten. She could no longer see and became a prisoner to her thoughts.

Her father was still missing... Evie had fallen ill... Her mother was wounded and lost somewhere up ahead...

Blind, alone, and confused, Kala stepped into TynkerVille.

<u>24</u>

Kala entered TynkerVille for the very first time… We've been here before, do you remember? It's where our story first began.

Kala, Fin, and Harrison Druthers explored the splendors inside TynkerVille. The rivers of molten metal… the golden walls… the forest made of pure silver…

They enjoyed all of this until the Designer showed up and told them that the "Tour of TynkerVille" was actually something very different. It was, in fact, a competition called The TynkerVille Trial and the loser was going to be thrown down a sewer well!

This change of circumstances (and the locking of TynkerVille's massive doors) raised the tension in the room. All three contestants — Kala, Fin, and Harrison — now wanted to **survive** their first trip to TynkerVille. But parts of them also wanted to find the gorgeous, *one-of-a-kind Tynk that the Designer had hidden in his silver forest. That was, after all, how to win his competition.*

All of that, you should remember. But a few other things happened during Kala's first trip to TynkerVille that you should also know about:

· Fin kept true to his word and refused to speak to Kala.

· Evie also kept quiet, but not by choice. There was something seriously wrong with the Tynk: her shell was thumping and hot as a stovetop.

· Marley Mayfair didn't make it to TynkerVille's silver fence in time. At first, this seemed like a tremendous waste. But, considering the change in TynkerVille's tour, all the other "winners" soon considered her lucky.

So what happens next? After his speech, the Designer vanished into the trunk of a silver tree as a small pathway opened in his forest. With nowhere else to turn, Kala (carrying Evie), Fin and Harrison began walking down a path of silver trees.

***

The place Kala walked through was divine. There were hundreds of silver trees that reminded her of the yew tree in the Holloton Library. But Kala knew there was little time to stare at these wonders. Her mission was to find her mother and the rest of Aeverum. Then, she would search for her father.

Kala heard the Designer's heavy feet pacing somewhere deep in his forest. "Welcome to Stage One!" his voice shouted as a deep rumble came from underground. The forest's silver trees started shifting and swaying. Their limbs reorganized themselves, crisscrossing until they made a huge, metal net. A circular cage quickly formed right on top of Kala, Fin and Harrison Druthers, and trapped them.

"The only way out is my passkey! Find it and speak it to the forest," the Designer said. "My trees will only open for the right word."

The Designer let out a mad cackle. Then, his voice and his footsteps faded away.

"So this is it?" Kala mumbled. "He's just going to trap us in his forest?"

Harrison Druthers was also confused. He looked at the metal net above him, then dropped to his knees and traced the golden roots that rushed along TynkerVille's marble floor. He slipped a finger beneath one of them and pulled. The root gave way. It was a lever that could be turned in a clockwise circle.

"Huh," Harrison grunted at his discovery.

He wound the golden root and the ground beneath him trembled once more. A metal noise was rattling up through the trunks of TynkerVille's trees. The sound came from hundreds of metal chunks that started spouting into the air.

Kala threw her hands onto her head and waited to be crushed beneath the falling metal. But no such thing happened. The metal chunks were light and hollow; they fluttered to the ground with beautiful, golden flashes.

Kala squinted and realized what the "metal chunks" really were. They were hollowed-out Tynks whose outer wheels had been turned into wings. They sailed to the ground like the flying seeds of maple trees.

"Fantastic," Harrison Druthers said, staring up at the Tynks. "Just fantastic!"

The old man dropped his cane and started catching the falling Tynks. Fin followed suit.

Kala joined the party and caught a few Tynks herself. They were light as leaves and made from precious metals. But, turning the Tynks through her hands, Kala found no words inscribed on their shells… no passkeys or hidden, magic phrases.

Confused, Kala looked over at Harrison and Fin. They were both stooped over their Tynks, studying the metal gadgets closely. Had one of them found the Designer's passkey? Was Kala already falling behind in this strange competition?

"What did you find?" Kala asked, running over to Fin.

But Fin quickly shoved her away and scowled. He didn't seem ready to forgive Kala for following him over TynkerVille's fence. Kala fell onto her back and a metal tree root dug into her side. But her fall proved useful, because only from the ground could Kala see TynkerVille's secret.

The Tynks being pumped into the air weren't just falling at random. They were fluttering to the ground in a very particular way. They formed clusters as they fell. Together, these clusters spelled out two words.

"*Iron heart*," Kala breathed.

The Designer's passkey wasn't written on the Tynks. It *was* the Tynks.

"I found you," Kala whispered.

A few yards away, Fin heard Kala mumbling and followed her eyes into the air. "You found it!" Fin shouted, and without another word, marched to the edge of the silver cage and whispered, *"Iron heart!"*

These words were indeed the passkey. A hole flashed open in one of TynkerVille's tree trunks and Fin stepped inside. He completed the first stage of TynkerVille's Trial and was whisked away.

Kala was furious at how this all unfolded. She pulled Evie from her pocket and said, "Can you believe him? He pushes me to the ground, steals my passkey then leaves without saying goodbye." Kala settled down when she felt the heat still steaming from Evie's shell. "Are you feeling any better?" she asked.

"A little," Evie managed. "I think it's the Designer. When I get close to him, my insides burn up."

"He must have something under that cloak," Kala guessed. "Can you still feel my mother's fire?"

"I can't feel anything, Kala. It hurts too much."

"Hold on. We'll get out of here soon."

Kala moved towards the same tree that swallowed Fin, but before she spoke TynkerVille's passkey, she looked back at Harrison Druthers. The old man was still slumped over a Tynk.

"Hey, you're not supposed to look there," Kala said.

The old man didn't respond. In fact, he didn't move at all.

"Harrison, did you hear me?" Kala asked. "The passkey isn't on the Tynks. It's up in the air!"

Kala jogged over and saw Harrison's face. The old man's eyes had gone completely grey. They were sapped of their color by the spinning Tynk in his hands.

"You too?" Kala whispered.

She remembered the Duckworth girls and all the drained strangers she'd passed in TynkerVille's alleyways. Kala knew there was no hope of saving Harrison, so ran back to the forest's silver cage, spoke *iron heart*, and climbed into the hole that opened in a nearby tree trunk.

The hole closed around Kala and swept her into total darkness. Kala couldn't see anymore, but she could still feel. She was being carried away, whisked through the silver forest towards the next stage of TynkerVille's competition.

<u>25</u>

TynkerVille's trees were not just hunks of silver. They were each machines with cogs and gears turning inside their trunks. Kala was carried through one of these trees and out into the air above. There, she was tossed between silver branches and whisked above TynkerVille's forest.

High in the air, Kala searched the forest for some sign of her parents, Aeverum, or the Designer's one-of-a-kind Tynk. But, as far as she could see, there were only silver trees.

"Useless," Kala whispered.

The silver trees that carried her seemed to be listening. They opened a silver tunnel in their limbs and swept Kala down. She screamed as she plunged towards the ground, and screamed louder when she saw what she was falling towards. It was a horrible jumble of metal spikes.

"You're not useless," Kala said. "Don't throw me in there!"

Kala was tossed into a small hole that opened in the metal thorn bush. Once inside, Kala could hear a voice. It was screaming. Fin was screaming.

***

"I'm coming, Fin," Kala shouted. "Just wait!"

There was hardly any light inside the thorn bush, and when Kala tried running forward, she found a complicated path. There was metal everywhere and she could only move by twisting her body.

Kala wriggled towards Fin and looked for some way out of the steel bush. But it had no openings for anything larger than a rabbit, and worse, the contraption was *shifting* every few seconds.

Bronze wheels spun above Kala and steel pistons thumped beside her. A moment later, Kala ducked as a silver blade flew inches over her head.

"You'll kill me!" Kala cried.

She kept her eyes and ears peeled and tip-toed towards the sound of Fin's voice. Kala found him a minute later, wedged between two metal wheels. Fin's weight was pressing right onto the place where their teeth met, locking him in place.

"Don't move," Kala said. "You'll make it worse!"

Fin wheezed and tears streamed from his eyes. He gripped his walking stick as metal teeth ground into his stomach. Kala tried to help him, pressing against the weight of Fin's body, but the giant metal wheels hardly budged.

"You have to drop your stick," Kala gasped. "It's too heavy!"

Fin wheezed again but refused to drop his walking stick.

"Drop it!" Kala screamed.

Finally, Fin let go of the stick and the wheels that trapped him gave way. He spilled onto the ground and clutched his ribs. He swept his walking stick, and the bag strapped to its end, back into his possession.

"What do you have gold in there?" Kala asked.

"None of your business," Fin wheezed. "So what is this thing?"

"You could say *you're welcome*," Kala spat.

"We're supposed to find the Designer's Tynk," Fin went on. "So why does he keep locking us in these weird places?"

"There's more going on here than just Tynks," Kala said, remembering her mother's words. "There's something the Designer's not showing us."

There was more light in this part of the bush, so Kala studied the metal around her. She saw massive gears of bronze and fist-sized jewels that connected them. She saw golden rotors sweeping overhead. Intrigued, Kala pulled Evie from her pocket and, keeping her hidden from Fin, opened the toy's orb.

"That can't be right," Kala whispered.

Her eyes bounced from her Tynk to the metal bush. Kala traced Evie's gears with her finger, then drew flowing shapes into the air.

"What can't be right?" Fin asked.

"I think…" Kala stopped to check Evie's orb one more time. "I think we're inside a giant Tynk!"

***

"That's ridiculous."

Fin shook his head and laughed, but when he looked around, his smile vanished. Fin no longer saw a random mishmash of metal. He saw cogs, gears and rotors linked together. They were giant versions of the pieces that made Tynks move.

"That's why we can't find a way out," Kala said. "Because we're not *supposed* to climb out. If this is a Tynk, then we have to open it from the center."

"I've never actually opened one," Fin muttered.

"There's a cage-like thing in the middle," Kala said. "We can twist it open."

"Okay," Fin shrugged. "You lead the way."

Kala wound towards the center of the giant Tynk. She moved ahead of Fin and hid Evie's blue light from him. To Fin, Kala was merely using one of the hollow Tynks that had fallen from the sky, *not* a magic toy that had life and blue fire.

As she moved, Kala felt lightness sweep her body. She was not afraid of the silver blades or bronze pistons around her. She understood this contraption now, and where all its gears were supposed to be.

Kala moved deftly through the metal maze. Evie and the giant Tynk were both the same puzzle, and Kala entered a

143

trance as she whisked through them. Without thinking, she looked to the gears inside Evie and immediately knew where they'd be in the larger Tynk.

This trance continued until Kala noticed a flash of green coming from her palms. They were emerald flames — Kindler fires — seeping from Kala's hands.

"Woah!"

Kala stumbled and the spell was broken. When she regained her balance, the green fires were gone. Only scars and Evie were left in her hands.

It was nothing, Kala thought. *You're seeing things.*

"What's wrong?" Fin asked.

"I thought I saw a rotor swinging for us," Kala said quickly, shaking her head.

Without another word, she completed their journey to the center of the Tynk. There, as Kala hoped, she found a giant, mesh cage.

"So how do we open this thing?" Fin asked. He pounded his fist against the mesh, but it hardly budged.

"Twist it to the side," Kala answered. "Then flip it open."

Together, Kala and Fin pushed on the upper half of the mesh and felt it slide to the right. The cage, just like the one inside Evie, moved until a loud and satisfying click could be heard. Then, Kala and Fin pushed up and watched the top half of the giant Tynk flip open. Light streamed in and the gorgeous limbs of TynkerVille's trees could be seen once more.

"You know this doesn't mean anything," Fin said as

brightness hit him. He rubbed his sore ribs and started climbing. "You're on your own again."

"Fine," Kala said.

She watched Fin climb out of the Tynk and back into TynkerVille's forest, but didn't chase after him. Kala waited behind and stared into her palms. Were there really emerald fires simmering there? After all these years, had she finally found her Kindler flames?

No, Kala thought. *That's not how it works. You weren't reading stories. The flames weren't blue. It couldn't have been Kindler fire.*

<u>26</u>

Kala traced the lines and scars that filled her palms. She thought of giant Tynks, metal puzzles and emerald fires, and those made her think of her mother: Luana Blaise... Aeverum's keeper... the Kindler...

Startled, Kala looked up. How long had she been staring into her hands? Fin was long gone, ahead of Kala in the Designer's Trial.

Kala still didn't know what this strange competition was all about — *was she supposed to find a one-of-a kind Tynk or merely survive TynkerVille's forest?* — but knew she couldn't afford to lose. It was the only path she could see to her mother. Kala needed to get moving.

Fortunately, the Designer made her next steps rather easy.

Kala climbed out of the giant Tynk and found the forest's silver trees shifted to the side. They made a long, glimmering hallway that Kala chased down.

In her hands, Evie was still warm and silent. Kala had no idea where the Tynk's mysterious pain was coming from but knew that escaping TynkerVille was her best chance at solving it.

At the end of the Designer's path, about three hundred yards away, Kala found two trees. They were each full of Tynks that hung from silver branches like acorns. Beneath these trees were two large holes that led deep into the ground.

Looking up, Kala saw Fin. He was climbing one of the silver trees, plucking Tynks off its limbs and throwing them down into one of the holes.

"Stage Three is simpler than the rest!" a voice called from the forest. Kala realized it was the Designer. *"Harvest my Tynk tree before the other and learn the path to my Tynk!"*

Was this it? The first to harvest a tree would win TynkerVille's Trial? It sounded too easy, but Kala knew there was no time to second guess the Designer's words. When his voice faded away, she leapt onto the tree beside Fin and started pulling down Tynks.

Kala flew from limb to limb, tossing Tynks into the ground as she went. Every now and then, she looked over to Fin. He was given a head start in this competition but was quickly falling behind. Unlike Kala, he had not grown up climbing a sacred yew tree in the Holloton Library.

Kala continued harvesting her Tynk tree until something hot trembled against her hip. It was Evie, who shouted, "*Kala! Kala!*"

"Not now," Kala said. "I'm almost done!"

"*Kala, watch out!*"

Kala listened to her Tynk a moment too late. She looked down and saw Fin climbing the trunk of *her* tree. Fin realized he was not going to win this stage of the competition, so decided that Kala must lose. He grabbed her ankle and pulled down hard. He made Kala lose her grip on the slick metal tree and sent her falling to the ground.

Kala felt weightless as she plummeted from the Tynk tree. She watched Fin grow farther away. She crashed into the ground and felt her head bounce against marble.

***

The next things Kala felt were Evie spinning against her face and a tremendous headache. Everything was a hazy wobble as Kala pushed herself up from the ground. She felt something fall into her lap, the Designer's gorgeous, one-of-a-kind Tynk. Made of platinum and decorated with diamonds, it bled a faint, green smoke from its gears.

"Wake up, Kala," Evie shouted. "Wake up!"

Kala's head thumped as her sight slowly returned. She was lying on TynkerVille's marble floor. Fin was gone and the Designer was sitting on a nearby tree stump.

"Gwen Duckworth, you've made it through the Trials," the Designer said. "And you found my Tynk. You've won!"

But when Kala looked up, she saw that her tree was still full of Tynks. She never completed the third challenge and didn't remember finding the Designer's Tynk.

"What's happening?" Kala groaned. "Where's Fin?"

"He took a tumble."

"A tumble?"

"Yes, a bit of a fall."

Kala stared down the holes in TynkerVille's floor. They were both wide enough to fit a falling boy.

"Did you throw him?" Kala asked.

"I did not," the Designer answered. "Fin went under his own power. He was convinced something was waiting for him beneath TynkerVille."

"Is that where you're hiding my mother?" Kala growled. "What about Aeverum and my father?"

"Well, *Gwen Duckworth's* mother is sitting at her kitchen table. I'm also not sure Gwen would care much about Aeverum," the Designer said, smiling. "*Kala Blaise* on the other hand… she might care about those things."

Kala shuddered as the Designer spoke her name. It was impossible to think properly with the pain in her skull, but Kala knew she'd just given up her identity. She wasn't sure this even mattered. The Designer seemed to know everything about her.

Kala watched the Designer rise from his stump and move to a nearby tree. He took hold of a branch and wound it. It was like the key to a music box, and as it spun, TynkerVille's forest

149

opened.

"You knew I wasn't Gwen Duckworth," Kala said to the Designer. "I could tell at the gate. This whole time, it's like you've known I was coming here."

"I've known for weeks," the Designer said.

"*Weeks?* You've been following me?"

"No, not following."

"Then how could you know?"

"Your life is like this room, Kala. It's a puzzle that I control." The Designer stopped winding his silver branch. "That's how this all began. A wounded Kindler... Colin McNair showing you a Tynk in the library... Each step of your life was a move planned by me."

"You can't just control me like that," Kala said. "I'm not one of your machines."

"No, but Evie is."

Kala pulled her Tynk from her pocket. "How do you know my Tynk's name?"

"How do I know you drained the Duckworth twins? How did I make sure you knew one of the Trial's winners in the first place? You're not feeling so well in here, are you Evie?"

Evie tried to speak, but a low and whining screech was all that came from her shell.

"Show her," the Designer commanded. "Show Kala the piece that doesn't feel right."

"Evie, what's he talking about?" Kala asked.

Evie let out another pained screech. Then, she spoke. "Open

me… To the right, there's a smooth disc. I don't think it should be there."

Evie tumbled her gears until one alone stuck up against its cage. Kala lifted the mesh away and found a smooth, blue disc.

"I'm surprised you didn't notice before," the Designer said. He reached into his cloak and pulled out a disc that matched Evie's. "Look, I've got one too! Evie was special long before she gained a voice. This Tynk was made *just* for you, Kala."

"What does that mean?" Kala shouted. "Hey, stop that!"

She heard her voice twice. Once as it left her mouth, then a second time as it rang from the disc in the Designer's hand.

"It's a new alloy I've been working with. It uses vibration to transport sound. It's been useful for all the announcements." The Designer flipped his smooth disc between his fingers. "This one captures the sound around Evie and communicates it to me. That's why Evie's been ill. She's too close to her receiver."

"You could hear everything?" Kala said.

"Of course," the Designer answered. "I've been planning all of this, just for you."

Kala looked down at Evie.

"Did you know?" she whispered.

"Not that he was listening," Evie said. "I couldn't have known, Kala!"

"You were his tool," Kala said. "He used you the whole time. He led me here."

"I'm me," Evie struggled. "No one controls me!"

"You're wrong. He controls you."

Evie couldn't speak anymore. She screeched in pain as her blue fire flickered and faded.

Kala turned back to the Designer.

"Why didn't you just carry me here when I was knocked out in the library?" she asked. "If all you wanted was me, why use my Tynk? It's too complicated."

"You needed to experience my competition," the Designer said. "You needed to find your Kindler fire."

"You saw that?" Kala gasped. She felt a familiar, emerald tingle rush to her palms.

"Your fire was as green as a caterpillar's flesh," the Designer said. "Clear as a smokeless diamond. Yes, I saw it."

The Designer turned his tree branch further. The forest's silver tree limbs curled away so that Kala could see up and inside of TynkerVille's large tower. It held an awesome network of gears, just like the ones that made Evie but hundreds of times the size. They were fixed into roots that stretched deep underground.

"That's a nice machine," Kala said. "But I don't see my parents up there."

"If all goes to plan, you'll have your Kindler back," the Designer said.

"What plan? What do you want with my family!?"

"I'll admit, things have gotten messy," the Designer sighed. "But you'll have it all back — your mother and Aeverum — once you answer a few questions."

"I'm not answering anything," Kala spat.

"Yes, you are," the Designer growled, flexing the metal veins in his neck. "What did you see during my Trial? What do you think of your competitors, Fin and Harrison?"

"I'll answer," Kala grumbled. "But I want to see my mother when I'm done."

"I promise you will."

Kala sat and thought for a moment. "Well, Harrison and Fin didn't see what they were supposed to see. The message in the air, the big Tynk... Harrison and Fin couldn't see the big things happening around them."

"That's right," the Designer said. "Life is a curious thing. There's far more happening than what's just in front of our eyes... Tell me more about Fin."

"He was the first person I met in TynkerVille," Kala said, rubbing the lump on her head. "But you probably know that already."

"And would you say that you *know* Fin?"

"I thought I did. But then he yanked me out of a tree."

"That's right... What about Harrison Druthers?"

"Harrison's drained now. He doesn't matter anymore," Kala answered.

"That's the lesson, Kala. There is darkness inside all of us," the Designer said. "Fin was overwhelmed by his darkness and hurt you. Harrison was saved from that part of his mind."

"What do you mean *saved?*" Kala asked.

"There's a line between madness and sanity," the Designer

153

said. "We're all capable of stumbling over it. We can all slip into the terrors in our minds."

Kala thought of a raging fire, a scorched library and the burns on her mother's face.

"Some of us can stay afloat," the Designer said. "I believe you're one of those people, Kala Blaise. The most important one of all."

"I'm not important," Kala said. "I lost both my parents. I was born to build Aeverum, and I can't even do that."

"But you've changed," the Designer said. "You have your own fire now. We both saw it."

"It's not supposed to be green," Kala whispered.

"Perhaps it's a new sort of fire," the Designer went on. "For a new sort of Kindler. That's why we're here... If you could save just one person from the madness in their mind, would you do it Kala?"

"You never said what *save* means. Does that mean drain people like Harrison?"

The Designer paced a circle around Kala. "I know what you're thinking. You're remembering what your mother's told you about the brightness in your mind. I'm telling you that brightness is a small speck in a much larger void. Madness is always closer than joy. That's why you're here — *you* and no one else, Kala. Haven't you seen people that would be better off without their Imaginations?"

"Maybe," Kala answered. "I'm not sure."

"If you could stop Fin from throwing his only friend from a

tree, would you do it?"

"I might."

"I brought you here to save the world from itself, Kala. I wanted you to see, to *experience*, the madness inside all of us. I wanted you to discover the green fire that's always been inside you. But most of all, I want you to be our new Kindler." The Designer looked right into Kala's eyes. "You'll be a Kindler who understands there's more than just brightness and stories in our minds. There's chaos, betrayal and madness, too. Can you guide us forward, Kala? Will you save us from ourselves?"

The Designer started walking down his silver path. He made it fifty yards before his metal exoskeleton collapsed inward. The Designer was crushed dead in the time it takes to snap a finger. His body was left in a broken, bloody heap on the ground.

Another man stepped into his place. He walked towards Kala and spoke.

"Kala, will you be our Kindler?" asked Mortimer Blaise.

27

Kala sprinted through TynkerVille but stopped just short of her father. Mortimer was wearing a tattered shirt, and beneath it, there was a familiar exoskeleton made of bronze and steel. It was the same metal skeleton that the Designer had worn.

Kala couldn't bear to look at the metal man now. The Designer's body was contorted into horrible shapes and blood stained his grey cloak. His eyes were grey and dead.

Closing her eyes, memories flooded back to Kala.

She remembered the inferno that swept through the Holloton Library: a fire the Designer had started.

She remembered sprinting from the library, leaving her mother in the flames and chasing after her father.

Then, Kala remembered dashing through the forest beyond

Holloton. The ground was lit with a strange, green light as Kala watched life drain from her father's eyes, as the Designer broke Mortimer and carried him away. For the first time, it all came back to Kala.

"I thought TynkerVille stole you," she whispered.

"I'm sorry," Mortimer said. "It was important for you to think that."

There were still some hazel flares left in Mortimer's eyes and his hair was as wild as ever. The only difference in Mortimer seemed to be the metal shell wrapped around his body. It held him up and supported his broken bones.

"So TynkerVille didn't take you?" Kala asked.

"Take me?" Mortimer smiled. "I *built* this Kala."

"No, the Designer did."

Mortimer looked over to the crumpled man. "I found him in Holloton. He was almost completely drained, but there was something left inside him. Enough to follow my orders, but not enough to think freely."

"You controlled him," Kala said. "And shocked him when he didn't listen. Is he like Evie? I saw the metal in his ears. Is that how you hurt him?"

"I stopped his mind from being totally lost. That's the best way to think of it," Mortimer answered. "But the Designer's gone now. Look around, Kala. I've made every branch and root in this forest."

"You never came back for me," Kala said. "You didn't want to see me?"

Mortimer walked towards Kala and dropped to his knee with a metal thump. He lifted his daughter's chin with his thumb.

"Don't you see?" he said. "This is all for you, Kala. The Tynks were meant to show you what people *really* are. The Trial was for you to find your Kindler fire. You're ready Kala. Don't you see?"

"Ready for what?"

"To be Kindler! The one who understands the whole mind — all of its good and all of its bad."

"What about the old one?" Kala asked. "You hurt Mom. You killed our tree!"

"That wasn't what it looked like," Mortimer said.

He moved to another tree and wound one of its roots. This time, the gears inside TynkerVille's tower began shifting and turning. There was a metal orb at the tower's highest point. It opened and revealed a blue fire: Aeverum.

"I've made a new machine to replace the yew tree," Mortimer said, grinning madly. "I saved the fire, Kala. I kept it here just for you!"

Kala took one look at Aeverum then turned back to her father. "Is Mom up there, too?"

"Why don't we have a look?" Mortimer said.

His smile shrunk as he kept thumping his root up and down. Something glimmering came into view. It was a cage of pure silver that floated over TynkerVille's forest. It held Luana Blaise, still wrapped in her tattered cloak.

"Your mother can't think like you and me," Mortimer said. "She's happy to let people go mad as long as they listen to her ridiculous stories. She's selfish Kala, but I never meant to hurt her."

Tears watered in Mortimer's eyes.

"The world has to be balanced," he said. "Your mother only cares about one part of our minds. The world needed someone else — *me* — to look out for the rest."

"What do I have to do with all this?" Kala asked.

"You're the one who can unite it all. The good and the bad, the divine and the devastating. You're the Kindler we need, Kala. One who can let Imagination flourish in the strong and not burden the weak."

"What does that mean *not burden the weak*?" Kala asked. "Even if that green thing was my fire, it doesn't make me a Kindler."

Mortimer thought for a moment before speaking. "It means you would redistribute the world's Imagination as we see fit… you'd give it to the capable ones and borrow it from the rest. It would make you a good Kindler, not a selfish one. Anxiety, depression, mania — you would save the world from all of it, Kala."

"What about Mom?" Kala asked. "She's still Kindler. Not me."

"Once you find your fire, you *become* a Kindler," Mortimer answered.

"It doesn't work like that," Kala said. "I don't have Mom's

necklace and there can only be one Kindler."

Mortimer shook his head and brought Luana's cage a little closer. She was asleep and did not wake as Mortimer ran a hand along her silver cage.

"Your mother has fed you a life's worth of lies," Mortimer said. "She scolds you for not finding your Kindler flame, while keeping you from the experiences you needed to find it. She's made you a prisoner, but still, I will let her live and write her stories."

Mortimer finished grazing the silver cage and walked towards Kala. "We can be a family again. You, me *and* your mother. Would you like that?"

"Yes," Kala said. "I would."

Mortimer held out his hand and Kala took it. It was cold and riddled with metal veins.

"Will you be the Kindler we need?" Mortimer asked, curling his cold fingers around Kala's. "Will you take from those who aren't strong? Will you save them?"

"Does that mean they'll be drained?"

"It only means they'll be saved."

Kala looked to her mother, then back at her father. "I want to be together again."

"Then become my Kindler," Mortimer said.

Kala nodded and a crash erupted through TynkerVille.

Luana Blaise snapped awake and cast a thick rope of fire around her silver cage. She ripped the metal open and leapt outside, then cast her sapphire rope around Mortimer and cinched it tight. Pulling harder, Luana forced a horrible crack from deep inside Mortimer. His face writhed with pain as his exoskeleton shattered around him.

"Kala, get Aeverum!" Luana shouted.

But Kala made no move for the fire. She stood still and watched her parents fight. Luana closed her rope around Mortimer, who took hold of the flame and started pulling it with his metallic arms. Even broken, Mortimer was able to haul Luana towards the two holes in his marble floor.

"The fire," Luana struggled. "Kala, get the fire!"

Her blue rope started to evaporate, and because it came from within her, it drained Luana's life as it vanished. Weak and hollow, Luana fell to her knees and was dragged through TynkerVille. Mortimer reeled her in by her blue rope and cast her into the hole in the floor.

"No!" Kala screamed.

She heard the thuds of a tumbling body as Luana fell deep into the earth. She plummeted towards a dark place Kala could not see.

"You have to stay with *me*, Kala," Mortimer said, shattered and wheezing. "Heal me."

"You broke her," Kala whispered. "She needs to build Aeverum."

"Not anymore," Mortimer gasped. "You can do it, Kala. You can be our Kindler!"

"I'm not ready to be Kindler!" Kala screamed.

Mortimer cried out as Kala ran for the pit her mother had

161

fallen into. He crawled towards the nearest tree and snapped away one of its silver branches. This broke something inside TynkerVille's tower and Aeverum began streaming from its orb. The blue fire slowly vanished into the air.

"I've got your fire!" Mortimer howled. "I'll burn it away! You'll be empty — *all* of us will!"

Kala dove into the same hole that took her mother, but not before looking back at her father. Mortimer's face was full of hate and streaked with tears. He let out a horrible yelp as Kala disappeared into the ground.

Kala slid into the earth and looked up at TynkerVille. She could still see her father's tower and realized what Mortimer had done. He'd broken his tower on purpose. It was now a machine that slowly destroyed Aeverum.

Kala closed her eyes and listened to her father's howls. She heard something else as she fell, a low and unfamiliar voice.

"*Burn away,*" it said. "*Burn away.*"

28

Kala and her mother fell through a network of tubes that lived beneath TynkerVille. They were dark and slick and led to an underground world.

Kala still heard limbs tumbling and a pained moan coming from her mother. Luana's attack on Mortimer used a large supply of her Kindler fire and had left her terribly weak.

Kala thought of her father, too. She remembered the sound of his exoskeleton breaking and the hate that filled his eyes. Kala didn't think she knew Mortimer anymore. The man who used to build watches in a secret closet in a basement was long gone.

Soon, TynkerVille's network of tubes spit out Kala and Luana. They fell twenty feet more and landed on a patch of soft dirt. Kala struggled to catch her breath as Luana sprawled along the ground.

"Mom, are you okay?" Kala ignored the bruises on her legs and her throbbing headache. Her only concern was her mother. Luana was unconscious and swept by a hollow chill.

"Mom, wake up," Kala said, poking her mother's cold arm. "Say something. Can you hear me?"

"Join Mortimer?" Luana gasped. *"You were going to help him... steal Imagination?"*

"No, Dad said I could help people," Kala said. "Did you know he built TynkerVille? Did you know he wasn't stolen?"

"Of course I didn't know... But how could you... join him, Kala?" Luana slipped back into delirium.

Kala turned away from her mother and burned with shame. They found themselves inside a thick, metal cylinder that was as wide as Holloton's streets. This was where TynkerVille's tubes had brought them.

There were no shops underground. In fact, Kala wasn't sure she recognized *anything* about this place. She watched a ring of strangers form around her. Their faces were slick with grease. Their hands were covered in grimy mittens that stretched from their fingers to their elbows. Behind this filth, Kala saw many sets of wonderful, blinking eyes.

"No one comes from those tubes," a woman said.

"Why'd they send them different?" someone else asked. "Are they special?"

The circle of strangers tightened around Kala. She

scrambled to her mother's side and looked to the ceiling. Fixed in the tunnel's roof — carved beside candles that were locked in cages — Kala found a system of hatches. They were the ends of the tubes that ran beneath TynkerVille. All of these hatches were fastened shut, including the one that spat out Kala and her mother.

"Protect Aeverum… it cannot go out," Luana whispered. She was slipping in and out of consciousness. *"The fire's for everyone, Kala… Strong or weak… I can't build it anymore."*

Kala thought to answer her mother but was more focused on the ring of strangers closing around them. A man stepped out from the crowd. He had a grey beard and brilliant, amber skin. One of his eyes was hazel. The other was cloudy and grey.

"Back away!" he shouted. "It's the storyteller, don't you hear?"

The bearded man stepped a little closer and leaned down to Luana's side. "Listen to her voice," he said. "Just listen."

"What story should we tell?" Luana struggled. *"The Horse and the Magpie… or Stealing the Moon?"*

"Do you hear?" the stranger shouted. "It's her — the voice from the pipes!"

No one in the crowd seemed to agree. They scratched their heads and whispered in each others' ears.

"Don't any of you listen?" the bearded man went on. "The stories that come down the tunnels, haven't you heard them?"

"He's mad," someone said. "Hearing things that aren't even there!"

Murmurs swept the crowd as they took one last look at the bearded man, Kala and Luana before backing away. As they left, Kala saw the other things that lived inside this underground tunnel. There was a road, of sorts. Dozens of people strolled down this wide avenue, all covered in grease and dirt. There were also tables full of food and new Tynks.

"Come, this woman needs care."

Kala turned and found a wavering hand. It was the man with green and grey eyes. He wasn't much taller than Kala and his beard was a wonderful mottle of black and grey.

"I'm Willem," he said. "What happened to the two of you? They weren't lying, you know. Those aren't tubes people come down."

"I guess we got lost," Kala said.

Willem frowned at this. "Is the woman sick?"

"She's my mother. You can call her Luana. She just hasn't slept in a while."

"I have a place for that. It's not far," Willem said. "Have you felt your mother's skin? That chill isn't from lack of sleep."

Kala looked down at her mother and gulped. Luana was silent and seemed to have slipped into a deep hibernation. She let out a slow wheeze as Willem bent down and scooped her into his arms. At first, Willem was strained by the effort. But after a moment, his face wrinkled with worry.

"So light," he whispered. "She feels hollow."

Kala grimaced and looked to the ceiling. She hoped to find something that could help her, something from the world above. But all she found were metal hatches and caged red flames. Kala was trapped underground and her mother was fading.

<u>29</u>

Kala followed Willem through the tunnels beneath TynkerVille. She noticed something strange about the people here: none of them were holding Tynks. They walked with free eyes and free fingers.

Kala thought of the Tynk in her pocket. "Are you okay?" she whispered to Evie. "Are you still hurt?"

"Be quiet," Evie whispered back. *"Your father can still listen to us!"*

"We're so far below ground," Kala said. "I doubt his disc even works."

"I'm not risking it," Evie answered. She went silent and cold in Kala's hands.

Sighing, Kala tucked Evie back into her pocket and jogged

up to meet Willem. He walked ten yards ahead with a frigid Kindler in his arms.

"Willem, you said you could hear stories?" Kala asked. "They were coming through the tubes?"

"Just like music," Willem said. "A few days ago, I heard a faint mumble. I opened one of the hatches, and there it was… a story! A few of us started listening from then on. Your mother would speak every few hours, telling pieces of some tale. It was about a woman, I gathered, and some machine in the sky."

"*Flying From the Dirt*," Kala said. "Mom must have memorized it."

"She has a wonderful voice. It takes us places… places far away from here."

A smirk slid over Kala's lips. "So what is all this?" she asked.

"This is TynkerVille's *real* factory," Willem said. "Where all the Tynks get made. That big castle in Holloton is just for show."

Kala looked around and saw thousands of metal pieces collected in wooden buckets. They were all parts of Tynks, waiting to be assembled.

"I can tell you more once we get your mother into bed," Willem said. "This way, I'm down in Tube Six."

Willem left the large tube that Kala and Luana had fallen into, and turned down a smaller one that branched from it. This smaller tube had cubbies carved into its walls. They were stacked from floor to ceiling, were covered with green curtains and could be reached with a system of ladders. It looked something like the book stacks that used to curve up the Holloton Library's walls.

"I'm five up from the bottom," Willem said. "Give me a hand, would you?"

Together, Kala and Willem hoisted Luana up the ladder and into Willem's cubby. It was a small space with a mattress and a stack of blankets. There was nothing else — no change of clothes, books or food.

"Wait with her while she sleeps," Willem said. "Oh, I forgot to ask… What do you call yourself?"

"Me? I'm Kala. Kala Blaise."

A smile poked through Willem's beard. His teeth were brilliant and only one of them was missing.

"There's a group of us," he went on. "We've been waiting for another story from your mother. You've got friends down here, Kala Blaise. Your mother made sure of it."

With that, Willem climbed back down to the floor of Tube Six. "Do you need food?" he called up from the ground. "I can grab my share early if you want?"

"We're not hungry," Kala said. "Will you be back soon? What do I call this place?"

Willem shrugged. "It has some fancy name… *Matricallary* or some nonsense like that. Most people just call it the Factory — it's easy enough to remember. There are a few doctors down here. I'll find one of them."

Kala nodded to Willem and watched him disappear into the tube's crowds. Then, she watched her mother drift back into a deep slumber. There was no glimmer in Luana: no blue magic dripping from her fingers.

"You won't leave me, will you?" Kala whispered.

She curled against her mother and thought of their old library. She thought of the glorious tree that once stood in its center, too.

***

Kala fell asleep beside her mother but didn't rest for long. She was woken by a high-pitched whine that came from Evie. The Tynk was firing her gears at a torrid pace.

"What's going on?" Kala grumbled.

"I'm spinning so your father can't hear us," Evie said. "It's loud inside me. Louder than our voices, I think."

"Relax, Evie. I think we're okay down here."

"I can't relax."

"You didn't know my father could hear us. You couldn't have known."

"I should have felt the disc," Evie said. "What if you had an extra bone in your chest? You wouldn't just forget about it."

Evie rolled out from Kala's pocket. "I've been thinking," she said. "I want you to take the extra gear out. I want you to destroy it."

"No way. Remember the last time you gave me a gear? It hurt you."

Luana shifted in her sleep and Kala threw her hands over Evie. Kala waited a moment, hiding Evie's light, before unwinding her fingers.

"What was that for?" Evie asked.

"Mom doesn't know about you," Kala said. "She's not so big on Tynks."

"*Not so big?*"

"Mom doesn't need a surprise right now. You'll meet her eventually."

Indeed, Luana Blaise was weakening by the hour. Her skin was pale. Her wooden Kindler necklace now weighed her down.

"Kala, I want the disc out," Evie whispered. "As long as it's there, your father owns me. I have to be me — just Evie — even if I'm missing a piece."

Kala hesitated a moment, then slowly cracked open Evie's shell. She saw the Tynk's cage and the mess of blue gears behind it.

"I'm going to hold the extra gear up," Evie said. "You need to lift my cage and pull it out."

"You promise this won't hurt?" Kala asked.

"Promise," Evie said.

Kala's fingers started trembling. She remembered the hiss of fire that came from Evie the last time she lost one of her gears.

"Go on," Evie said. "Take it now, Kala!"

Kala pulled open Evie's cage and ripped away the smooth, metal disc. But the gear didn't come away cleanly — it brought a brass cog and a golden rotor with it. Other pieces of metal were warped as a flash of fire erupted from Evie. She let out a terrible whine as she tried to move her gears.

Something was wrong with them. Their connections had been broken.

"Now your father can't hear us anymore," Evie said. But her voice had lost everything that made it splendid. There was no music anymore, just an uneven thump of metal.

Kala tried to set Evie's gears back in place, but many of them had been warped. Evie's core started to flicker and fade. Her light went out and left Willem's cubby in darkness. Kala sunk into the wall as Evie went cold in her hands. She closed her eyes and felt the chill creeping from her mother.

"Why is everyone leaving me?" Kala asked.

No one answered her.

30

Time was lost in the tubes. There was no sunlight below the ground, just the dim haze of candles. Kala was woken by a rustle and had no idea what time it was. Luana and Evie were still sleeping beside her as Willem swept aside their cubby's curtain.

"I brought Ana with me," Willem whispered. "She studies herbs. Not quite a doctor, but she'll help your mother."

A young woman with copper hair waited below the cubby. She carried a small, linen bag that was full of jarred herbs.

"I love your mother's stories," Ana said. She spoke quietly and made sure that no one except Willem and Kala could hear her voice.

"Your mother's not... how should I say... *typical* down

here," Willem said. "We don't have books and stories. Most people are suspicious of them."

"Suspicious?" Kala said.

"The people in these tubes have come from all over the world," Willem answered. "They've brought their superstitions with them. You'll learn."

Willem helped Kala down to the ground as Ana, carrying her bag of herbs and seeds, took her place at Luana's side.

"I don't think basil and thyme are going to help her," Kala muttered.

"You can trust Ana," Willem said. "She'd never harm your mother."

"I'm not sure anyone could do more harm," Kala sighed.

She climbed back up and made sure the curtain to Willem's cubby was closed. Now, only a sliver of light shone on Luana and Ana.

"Are you two hiding from someone?" Willem asked.

"It's just better if everyone forgets we're here," Kala said.

"I understand," Willem sighed. "Everyone's running from something down here."

Kala, who still carried Evie in her pocket, and Willem walked towards the Factory's main tunnel. It was full of bustling crowds and buckets full of gears and Tynks. As she walked, Kala looked up at the hatches notched into the ceiling. She studied their heavy locks.

"So how do we get out of here?" Kala asked.

"There's always the way you came in," Willem said,

glancing at the roof.

"We can't climb those tunnels, they're too slippery."

"That's correct."

"So how do we get out?"

"You don't."

Willem saw fear dance in Kala's eyes and let out a long sigh. "We all took the plunge, including you," he said. "It's a one-way ticket. There *is* no way out from the Factory."

"But there has to be," Kala sputtered. "My mom has medicine up there!"

"Unless you grow wings, there's no way back," Willem said. "I'm not saying that to hurt you, Kala. It's just the way things are."

Kala thought of Aeverum bleeding in a tower somewhere above her. That vanishing blue fire and Luana Blaise were the only things that could save each other...

Kala swiped a Tynk from one of the tube's buckets and watched it spin. It gave her some comfort and took her mind off her mother and Aeverum. But Willem quickly batted the toy away and tossed it back into the bucket.

"You don't take *anything* down here," Willem said. "It's not the way we do things."

"It was just sitting there," Kala groaned. "There's hundreds of them."

"That Tynk was where it's supposed to be."

Willem walked further down the Factory, and for the first time, Kala studied the underground community's layout. The

Factory was a system of tubes shaped into a massive wheel. There was a curved central tube and many secondary tubes that branched from it. Those held the cubbies that everyone slept in.

"There's a contract down here," Willem went on. "Everything has to be in balance. A certain amount of people make a certain amount of Tynks and get a certain amount of food. It keeps the Factory in order."

"But all I did was take a Tynk?" Kala said.

"Even little things can throw off the balance. Every cog, every rotor, every *Tynk* — they're all accounted for. Right down to the chunks of ore that made them."

"So you can't own anything down here?" Kala asked. "You just get food and water?"

"And a bed," Willem said. "But that's all we need, Kala. The people down here don't come from Holloton or places like that. They want simpler things."

"So *all* you do in the Factory is make Tynks?"

"There are other jobs, but that's the end goal."

"It's a prison," Kala said, looking around. "You can't get out. You have to *work* all day."

"All some people want is a hot meal and a private place to sleep at night. It's not for you to judge, Kala."

The air grew warmer, and soon, a film of smoke could be seen rushing along the Factory's ceiling. There was noise, too, a thin clatter sounding in the distance.

"This is why we're all here," Willem said. "This is where the

Tynks gets made."

He pointed to a large opening in the Factory's inner tube. It was a long, downward sloping tunnel full of blinding light. There was a track that brought empty, wooden containers to the bottom of the tunnel. When they came back up, they were filled to their brims with brand new Tynks.

Kala ran a hand over her pocket. She felt Evie, cold and unmoving.

Maybe I can fix you, Kala thought. *You just need some new parts.*

"Can we go down there?" Kala asked Willem. "I want to see how the Tynks get made."

"Not unless you work there."

"Can I just peek down the tunnel? No one will notice."

"They *will* notice."

Kala slipped her hand into her pocket. She ran a finger along Evie's orb and pictured the exact gears she'd plucked away. She held them in her mind and started running. Willem tried to grab Kala's arm, but she wriggled free.

Everyone's eyes instantly fell on Kala. She leapt into the bright tunnel and caught a ride in one of its empty carts. Kala looked behind her but could not see Willem. He refused to run through the Factory.

"I can fix you," Kala said, pulling Evie from her pocket. "Then we'll find a way out of here... we'll bring Mom back to Aeverum."

Evie let out a terrible screech.

"What was that?" Kala asked.

Another clatter of metal came from Evie.

"Don't talk," Kala said. "I'll find you more gears."

Kala looked down at the flood of light approaching her. It was riddled with sound, steam and smoke as black as coal. This was the real factory, where all the world's Tynks were made.

31

Kala leapt from her cart into a cloud of steam. She rolled into a massive cavern that held an endless supply of machinery. It was the space inside the Factory's inner ring: a huge, underground dome where Tynks were made.

There was a massive cloud of smoke that hung below the dome's ceiling. Beneath this, Kala saw machines of every kind, all slick with grease and powered by fire. They had children zipping through them, dashing between mazes of thumping gears.

Below the noise of the machines, Kala heard something in her hands.

"Do you hear me, Kala?" Evie wheezed. "I sound *horrible*."

"I can fix you," Kala said. "I just have to find the right parts."

"There's no fixing me," Evie sputtered. "Your father made me special. They won't have the right pieces down here."

"They'll have something. We'll make it work."

"The rotor was one thing. But a talking Tynk!?"

These words didn't come from Evie. They came from a boy who stood just feet from Kala. He had a clumpy, linen bag slung over his shoulder and a wicked grin on his face.

"I know TynkerVille didn't sell you *that*," Fin said.

When Kala saw Fin, she was not startled or confused. She was furious. "Is that all you have to say?"

Kala jumped on Fin and tackled him to the ground. Fin laughed at first, until his linen bag tore open beneath his weight. All his objects spilled onto the ground: a pair of broken dice, a hat big enough for a toddler, a glass bottle filled with clear goop, and more.

Fin leapt on top of these useless objects. He ran the bottle of clear jelly through his fingers.

"You broke my bag," Fin muttered. "Kala, you broke it!"

"So what?" Kala screamed. "You pushed me out of a tree! Remember that?"

Fin kept pulling in his lost items. One by one, he took count of them, then placed them back into his bag.

"Don't you ever touch my things," Fin said. He held his bag against his chest, sealing its rip.

"No, you don't get to say that!" Kala growled. She lifted her hair and revealed the welt from her fall. "You're going to tell me why you're down here — why you threw me from a *tree* —

or I'll burn that bag and everything in it!"

At this, Fin went quiet. He brought a finger to his lips and looked around. Kala followed his eyes and saw that the Factory's workers had all come to a stop. They stared at Kala and Fin.

"Not now," Fin whispered. "Not *here*."

Sweat dripped down Kala's neck. Carefully, she helped Fin up from the floor and they moved towards the carts heading out of the cavern. As they left, Kala and Fin heard the crash of machines resume and whispers rising behind them. They were rumors about the boy and the girl who had broken the Factory's peace.

"You shouldn't have done that," Fin whispered.

"No, *you* shouldn't have done that," Kala said, pointing at the lump on her head.

"I guess I'm sorry."

"You guess?"

"I didn't feel bad at first. Now, maybe I do a little bit."

"Thanks," Kala muttered. "So why did you come down here? You were acting strange the whole time we were in TynkerVille."

"You weren't so normal yourself," Fin said.

When their cart reached the top of its track, Kala and Fin leapt into the Factory's main tunnel and looked behind them. No one had followed them. All the Factory's workers were making Tynks again.

"I might have found something... a place where we can talk

about everything," Fin said. "But I can't take you there yet. We need to be quiet for a while, until people forget about us."

"Are you staying in one of those cubbies?" Kala asked. "Which tube are you in? I'll come find you."

"I'm not staying here," Fin said, and started walking away.

"But there's nowhere else to stay!" Kala shouted.

"Keep your voice down," Fin hissed. "I'll be back for you soon."

Fin slipped into the Factory's crowd. Kala lost sight of him as questions rolled to the tip of her tongue. She wanted to know where Fin was staying if not *here* in the Factory. She wanted to know why he cared so much about those useless things that spilled from his bag.

But as Kala looked for a final glimpse of Fin, she felt the hair on her forearms raise. She realized everyone was staring at her again.

"I hate this place," Kala muttered.

She walked through the Factory's main tunnel until she was confident no one was watching her. Then, Kala retraced her steps back to Tube Six. There, she found a small crowd. A dozen people were huddled along the tube's wall, looking up to a lone speaker. She was teetering from the edge of her cubby and struggling to read a story.

It was Luana Blaise.

32

Kala walked behind the crowd and looked up at her mother. There was some life in Luana's eyes. She held a thin stack of paper, a story she was slowly moving through.

"Beautiful voice," Ana said to Kala. The healer smelled of black pepper and tea leaves. Her eyes dazzled as she looked up at Luana.

"You should have heard her before," Kala whispered back.

It was true, Luana was not telling stories like she once did in the Holloton Library. Her eyes were fluttering beyond her control, switching between her papers and delirium. She mumbled some story about an antelope who saw the moon falling through the sky, but soon, Luana fell to her weakness. Her words started to slur, and she wavered at the edge of her bed.

Kala dashed up the tube's ladder and kept her mother from falling. She rested Luana back in bed and took the crumpled story from her hands.

"Lie down," Kala whispered. "Rest, Mom."

Luana closed her eyes and bled warmth. She nestled into the corner of Willem's cubby and left Kala to the crowd below. They didn't seem so concerned with Luana. They cared more about the end of her story.

"What happens to the deer?" someone muttered.

"It's not a deer, it's an antelope," another said.

"Same thing. Does the moon fall on it?"

Kala smiled as she looked down. She wondered if these were the people Willem spoke of, the friends who listened to Luana's stories as they came down through the Factory's tubes.

But soon, Kala's joy fizzled away. She could feel the stares of everyone below her. She felt the weight of the story in her hands.

"Will you finish it?" someone called up.

"Me?" Kala said.

"Someone's got to finish it."

"I… I don't do stories," Kala said. "Maybe I can try reading it. But I can't *tell* it."

"What's the difference?"

"I don't know, there just is."

Kala felt her stomach lurch. She shuffled her mother's

papers and felt sweat drip from her palms.

"It's called *The Antelope and the Moon,*" Kala said. "Maybe I'll just start from the beginning, okay? It says this is the tale of an antelope and her moon. But I guess you already knew that from the title."

Kala feared her words would sound nothing like her mother's. There was no rhythm to her voice. It was a crackling squeak that struggled to reach the ground.

"So umm… the antelope found no friends around her pond," Kala went on. "All she could do was look up. But when she did, she saw… she saw the moon falling through the sky!"

As she moved through the story, Kala started to feel more comfortable with its words. She followed her mother's handwriting like a stone path, leaping from each syllable to the next. Kala strung these sounds into words and sentences, and soon, into meaning.

"The antelope watched her moon come crashing down. It filled the sky with white light, until it collapsed into a small, yellow point. The antelope walked towards that yellow point and realized the moon wasn't very big at all. It was lonely in the dark and had come down from the sky to find a friend."

Kala's words were crisp and clear now. She didn't dwell on this. She kept reading.

"The antelope carried the moon through the plains. She showed it water and grass and trees. And when morning came, the moon returned to its spot in the sky, but not without making a promise. The moon would return to the ground once a year, or whenever it needed a friend."

Friend. Kala exhaled as she read the last word. She flipped Luana's papers over and back again but found nothing more to read. The story's spell was broken. Kala looked down and saw familiar faces. There was Ana, Willem, and off to the side, Fin.

"Splendid."

A lone word slipped into Kala's ear. It was her mother, using all the strength she had left before she closed her eyes and fell back asleep.

"I was just reading," Kala whispered back.

After making sure her mother was fast asleep, Kala climbed down to meet her crowd. Fin was gone, but Willem, Ana and their friends remained. Each of them was luminous, a beacon of stories in the darkness of the Factory. Kala shook all of their hands, but stopped when she reached Willem.

"Just like your mother," he said. "Perfect!"

Willem's smile was the brightest thing in Tube Six. Kala noticed something in his eyes, particularly the one without any color. She thought she saw it twinkling in the dim light.

"How did you get two different eyes?" Kala whispered.

Brightness faded from Willem. "It was an accident. If you want to call it that."

"It was a Tynk, wasn't it?" Kala asked.

Anger flashed through Willem. "How could you... Yes, it was a Tynk. I threw the damned thing away before it got all of me."

"I'm glad it didn't," Kala said.

She stared into Willem's left pupil, hoping to see another flash of color. Had it really glimmered before? Could Kala's story have caused that flash?

"I can still see out the bad one," Willem said. "There's just something wrong with it. Empty, I guess… You and your mother can stay in Tube Six, by the way. I'll find another cubby. This way your commute won't be too far."

"Commute?" Kala asked.

"I found you and your mother jobs. Everyone needs to work in the Factory, Kala."

"When did you do that?"

"When you decided to run away and start a fight in the middle of the machines!" Willem tried to laugh but couldn't hide the disappointment in his voice. "I convinced some friends that we need a new sort of job, one that lets us all relax a little bit. You just passed your test, Kala. You and your mother are official Storytellers — the first we've ever had!"

"No, I can't do that!" Kala burst. It felt like she was sinking down to a place even lower than the Factory's tubes. "I read one story. That doesn't make me a storyteller."

"Well, you and your mother's names are in our accounting book next to the word *Storyteller*. It doesn't matter if you're supposed to be a Welder or a TubeSweeper. You're going to read stories, Kala — every night and there's no way around it. Now, grab some food and be back here in four hours. You've got your first *official* story and there's going to be a crowd to see it!"

Willem walked away as Kala went mute. She looked at the mighty green tubes surrounding her. They offered Kala no escape to the world above, and now, no escape from her fate.

33

Kala tried not to think of her new job. She climbed back to her mother and found her a touch warmer than before. Luana was now able to speak in a hoarse whisper.

"Wonderful voice," she managed. "I had no idea."

"I was just reading," Kala said. "It was your story, anyway."

"The words are a small part. The storyteller... the crowd... their bond. Those are what matter."

Kala shrugged and stared into her empty palms. She had still not seen a hint of green fire since it appeared in TynkerVille.

"Have you brought someone with you?" Luana asked. "Aeverum, I can feel it."

"It's just me," Kala said. "There's no one else here."

Luana slipped her hand into Kala's pocket and pulled out Evie. She turned the Tynk through her hands and traced Evie's blue fire.

"What are *you*?" Luana asked. She found the seam in Evie's orb and started to twist it open.

"Careful, you'll hurt her!" Kala said.

"Her?" Luana asked.

"*Me.*"

Evie spoke in harsh jolts, but soon, her words smoothed.

"I used to be more than this," Evie said. "I wish you could have seen me then."

"Evie was made by our tree after the Designer hurt you," Kala said. "She helped me find you, but we didn't know Dad put an extra gear inside her. It let him hear everything, so Evie made me take it out… She was hurt."

"It made me *this*." Evie's words screeched when they hit the air. "Take my fire, Mrs. Kindler. You'll use it better than me."

"Just don't hurt her, Mom," Kala said. "I know you hate Tynks, but this one tried to help you."

Luana opened Evie's orb and studied her blue gears. She didn't take any of Evie's fire, but merely watched as Aeverum wound its way through the Tynk.

"Maybe I was wrong about Tynks," Luana said. "I might have been wrong about a lot of things."

Luana's words brought Evie some life. She flared with sapphire and rolled a few laps around the cubby.

"I failed us," Luana went on. "I failed *you*, Kala."

"That should have been my hundredth story, not my first," Kala said. "If I realized who the Designer really was — if I had my Kindler fire — we wouldn't be here right now. You wouldn't be dying."

Dying. The word hung in the air between Kala and Luana.

"I am dying, Kala. But you can't save me, even if you do have your fire. I need more flame than the others — I need *Aeverum*. My bond with the fire is like yours to blood." Luana sighed. "I can feel Aeverum bleeding, Kala. Your father's destroying the fire, and me along with it."

Kala eased her hand between her mother's palms.

"Do you think he'll come after us?" she asked. "Do you think he's still in there, behind all that metal?"

"I'm sure your father started plotting the moment I broke him. But he's not what we need to worry about right now," Luana said. "I've known thousands of people from my stories Kala, and yet I don't know the one who matters most. I always saw you as the next Kindler. I never saw you as my daughter."

A tear trickled down the corner of Luana's eye. It slipped into her hand and between Kala's fingers.

"I've placed an impossible weight on you," Luana said. "I've crushed you with it since you were born. The world will sort out its fires when I'm gone, but I'm afraid it won't sort out *you*. Can you forgive me, Kala?"

"I'll bring you to Aeverum," Kala said. "We'll heal you, then we won't have to worry about—"

"I'm not asking to be saved, Kala. I'm asking to be forgiven."

Kala looked up from her damp palms. Her mother looked so old now, so frail. Life clung to Luana's bones.

"Only if you forgive me, too," Kala said.

She fell into her mother's lap. Evie rolled between them, and together, they were a family of three.

34

Luana's warmth kept slipping away and Kala realized that the way back home — the way to Aeverum — would not be found in Willem's cubby. She left her mother and carried Evie to the floor of Tube Six. There, Fin was waiting.

"Nice voice," he said. "It gets deeper when you read."

"You're back already?" Kala asked.

"Well, I was thinking and... maybe we can talk about something."

"I thought you were waiting until everyone forgot about us?"

"Will you just follow me?" Fin said. "I think you might understand."

"Fine. But I need to be back in a few hours."

Fin smiled and led Kala back into the Factory's main tunnel. The tube felt different now, darker and tighter, as Kala remembered her mother's words.

Was Mortimer really broken? What was he planning now?

"We have to be fast," Fin said. "No one can see us."

"Fast about what?" Kala asked.

Fin placed his hip against a large bucket of Tynks, and after a quick glance around, nudged it to the side. A hidden crack in the wall was revealed.

"Inside, *now!*"

Fin grabbed Kala's arm and yanked her into the hole. He pulled the Tynk bucket back into place and sealed them both in darkness.

Kala pulled Evie from her pocket and let her blue light fill the space around them. They were inside a narrow channel, a passage carved into the dirt just outside the Factory's tubes.

"I was walking the other day and felt a breeze around my ankles. One push later and I found this," Fin said. "So where'd you get the talking Tynk?"

"Her name's Evie," Kala said. "And she's a long story."

"We've got time. No one will find us here."

"*You've* got time," Kala said. "Go on, why'd you bring me here?"

Fin rolled his eyes. "Fine, don't tell me. We're going to crawl a little while. It opens up eventually."

"I'm not crawling anywhere."

"Oh, come on."

Fin crawled ahead, and after a loud humph, Kala followed him. They moved on their hands and knees until the dark passage grew and allowed them to stand.

"This must be where they brought all the pieces down. The ones that made the Factory," Fin said. "TynkerVille probably sealed all the chambers when they were done. They must have forgotten one."

"Does anyone else know about this?" Kala asked.

"Only you. But I don't think the others would care much. They're happy down here, happier than anyone I ever saw in Holloton."

"Is that where this leads?" Kala asked. "Is there a way home?"

"Not that I've found," Fin sighed. "It just leads to more and more tunnels. But there's something up here I want to show you."

Fin led Kala further down the way, until it turned sharply upward. There was a ladder that climbed up and into the dark. Kala cupped her hands around Evie and focused her light, but still, she could not see the ladder's end.

"You're really just going to carry around a talking Tynk and not tell me where you found it?" Fin asked.

"My name is Evie," the Tynk said.

"And she prefers sapphire to blue," Kala added.

"Alright, *Evie*. I'm guessing they didn't make you in the Factory?" Fin asked.

"I was made in Aeverum, in the flame of the Kindler

herself!" Evie cried.

But her voice was still a jumble of steel. Embarrassed, Evie went quiet and her blue light dimmed.

"What's a Candler?" Fin asked.

"Start climbing and we'll tell you," Kala sighed.

They started up the underground ladder, and Kala told Fin the story of Kindlers. He learned about libraries, blue fires, TynkerVille's plan and Mortimer's disappearance.

"So the Designer was controlled by your father the whole time?" Fin asked once Kala was done. "You didn't notice? I think I would have noticed."

"It wasn't really my father," Kala said. "He was part machine and part Dad… I'm not sure how much of each."

"Weird," Fin sighed. "And I guess your mother's not feeling too well without her fire?"

"I need to get her back to Aeverum. That's why I need a way out."

"I don't know if there is one, Kala. Maybe you'll see things differently than me. I get distracted up here."

"Distracted by what?"

"You'll see."

The ladder finally came to an end and spit the climbers out into another tunnel. This one was different than the tubes in the Factory. It was made of crumbling stone and filled with pools of glowing liquid. All of them smelled awful.

"Welcome to Holloton's sewers," Fin said.

"Gross," Kala muttered.

She moved towards one of the glowing pools and hovered her foot over it.

"Don't touch!" Fin said. "It'll burn you."

"What is it?" Kala asked.

"Garbage, I think. Everything from Holloton runs down to here. The puddles are all a little different, but none of them do anything good."

"Are you studying them or something?" Kala pointed to the wall of the sewer, where dozens of glass bottles sat filled with liquids and jellies. They were similar to the one that spilled from Fin's bag in the Tynk factory.

"Is that your new hobby?" Kala chuckled. "Collecting garbage?"

"It's not like that."

Fin turned away and Kala saw his cheeks burn red. He led Kala and Evie through more crumbling tunnels, until a shard of light could be seen in the distance. It came from above the ground, and once she saw it, Kala ran for it.

She sprinted around puddles of trash and dodged loose stones that tumbled around her. She didn't hear Fin screaming for her to stop. She didn't hear a familiar moan sounding from ahead. Kala only saw the beam of light. A way home, she hoped...

***

"Wait!" Fin shouted. "You'll scare them!"

Kala kept racing towards the light. It meant a way out, a way to bring her mother back to Aeverum. When she reached the end of the tunnel, Kala found a massive chamber. An odd mountain of dirt sat in its center, and around it, there were dozens of drained people. Their eyes were totally grey. They slouched against the ground and moaned.

"What's in there?" Evie asked. "I can't feel any fires."

"There are none," Kala said. "Fin, what is this place?"

Kala remembered the fog that slipped from her father's eyes and the hazel wisps that bled from the Duckworth twins.

"They don't hurt anyone," Fin said. "This is what I wanted to show you. I thought you might understand."

"Understand what?"

"I saw you with your mother," Fin said. "I thought…"

"My mom's sick, not *drained*," Kala said. "Did you really think this was the same?"

"I… I can bring you back down," Fin sputtered. "Maybe this was a bad idea."

Fin seemed to shrink as he walked away. But Kala caught him by the shoulder and spun him back around.

"No," she said. "Show me why we're here."

Fin walked past Kala into the chamber. He moved around the large mound of dirt, where empty TynkerMeal containers were strewn all over the ground. There were skins of leather, too, some with water dribbling from their spouts.

"What is this place?" Kala asked, but still, Fin wouldn't answer.

He kept walking towards the wall of the cavern, where two people sat huddled together: a man and a woman, both about the age of Kala's mother. Fin stooped down and lifted the woman's hand.

"Meet Henry and Rose," he said. "My parents."

Fin grabbed a half-empty TynkerMeal and tipped it open. Dried fruit fell onto his mother's mouth, until she opened her lips and took a weak gulp. Fin did the same for his father. He fed his parents.

"I needed to find where TynkerVille sent them," Fin said. "That's why I pushed you in the castle... I just needed to win. But I always thought TynkerVille would have a secret building where they sent all the drained. It was the sewers the whole time... It can't be good for selling Tynks if drained people are walking around, so they built that tunnel and threw a bunch of dirt down it. Then, they started throwing people down."

Kala saws dozens more drained people just like Fin's parents. Nearly all of them were adults, stripped of their Imagination and tossed underground.

"So TynkerVille throws them food, and they're just supposed to take care of themselves?" Kala asked.

"I don't think TynkerVille wants them to die." Fin tipped another TynkerMeal down his father's throat. "They just want people to forget them and sell as many Tynks as they can."

"Have you been taking care of all these people?" Kala asked.

"Only since I found them. They can still eat and drink on their own — they're not totally gone."

Something flickered through Fin's eyes.

"Mom and Dad got drained early on," he said. "I took care

of them for as long as I could, but when we lost our house it got a lot harder. One day, I came back and they were just gone. I heard rumors that TynkerVille was sending them somewhere underground, but I couldn't get into the sewers. I'm sorry I hurt you, Kala. I just needed to know where they were."

Fin reached into his linen bag and took out a glass jar of clear jelly. He threw it into a clearing and it erupted into a fireball when it hit the ground.

"Hey!" Kala shouted.

But the fire didn't grow. It simmered in place, warm and auburn.

"It gets cold in here," Fin said. "They can eat by themselves but they can't make fire."

"Is that why you have all those jars back there?" Kala asked.

"Sure," Fin muttered. "That's why."

He stooped down and nestled into the space between his parents. There, Fin closed his eyes and let a tear roll down his cheek. It glimmered in his roaring fire as his parents stared blankly ahead.

35

Kala and Evie left Fin with his parents. It was a time for family, not friends. Kala also knew she was needed back in the Factory; it was nearly time for her first "official" story to be read.

"Why do you think Fin brought us here?" Evie asked. "We can't help his parents."

Kala looked back at Fin. He whispered something into his father's ear and then his mother's. They said nothing in return, but still, Fin kept whispering away.

"I think he wanted someone to be alone with," Kala said.

She and Evie retraced their path through the crumbling sewers but found no other shafts of light or connections to the outside world. There was only darkness and the long ladder back to the Factory.

As she climbed down, Kala realized the ladder was no help for her mother. The shaft was much too narrow for anyone to carry Luana. Kala's only hope was finding another way out of the Factory, one that was wider and led all the way above ground.

Soon, Kala was back in the Factory. She snuck back into Tube Six and found ten people gathered there: Willem, Ana and their friends. Kala paid this crowd little attention and rose to meet her mother. Luana was huddled into a cold ball. The warmth she found during Kala's story had burnt away.

"How are you feeling, Mom?" Kala asked.

She brushed her mother's hair and felt it break in her hands. Luana groaned and tried to scratch her dried throat.

"Is it story time?" Luana asked. "For our new storyteller?"

"Maybe. It's hard to know what time it is down here," Kala said. "And don't call me storyteller. I'm only doing this until we get out of here."

"Once you start reading… people will gather. Stories don't care what time it is."

"Maybe *your* stories," Kala sighed. "Mom, I need to tell you something. Fin showed us this huge ladder. It leads to a cave that… well, it has light and some other stuff inside. But the light's coming from Holloton!"

"That's nice," Luana said.

"That's nice?" Kala asked. "Don't you want to get out of here? Don't you want to get back to your fire?"

"I'd like to hear my daughter tell a story first."

As Luana spoke, a small blue spark ignited in her hand. She hovered it over the stack of paper beside her and set it on fire.

"Stop it, put them out!" Kala shouted. She lunged for the papers, but her mother yanked them away. The blue fire grew, and a moment later, the stories were reduced to ash.

"I needed those!" Kala said.

She picked up a heap of warm ash and let it sift through her fingers. The words, sentences and stories were gone.

"They come from inside us," Luana said, placing a hand onto her chest. "Stories are carried in our bodies and given to others. They're real, but not because they're written on paper."

"Would you stop that?" Kala cried. "My life isn't one of your books! I can't tell my own stories, I can hardly read yours!"

"I believe in you, Kala. I believe in you now and I always have, even if it seemed like the opposite was true."

"A week ago you said I'm not a Kindler," Kala argued. "You wouldn't let me leave the house!"

"Just because I was a fool doesn't mean you're not ready to tell stories," Luana said. "Look how far you've come without me, Kala. You found me after I was taken. You made new life with the fire."

Kala pulled Evie from her pocket. "Yeah and look where's it gotten all of us. Trapped in a bunch of tubes while Aeverum's being burned away."

Luana reached for Evie and whispered to her. "Kala's going to tell a story now."

"No, I'm *not.*"

"You'll have to help her," Luana went on. "Be the warmth by her side… keep her going if she gets lost."

"Yes, Mrs. Kindler," Evie said. "But how will I know if she's lost?"

"You'll know," Luana said. "Our heads are big places, you'll have to keep Kala in the bright parts of hers." Luana turned to her daughter. "I tried to keep your father there… I remember feeling something heavy in his heart, growing each day. But Mortimer wouldn't take my help. He wouldn't fight his own head, Kala."

"Why did you tell me he was stolen if you weren't sure?" Kala asked.

"I couldn't have you thinking he just left. Had I known the whole truth, I'm not sure what I would have said."

"Do you think Dad's still in there?" Kala asked. "He's not drained. I saw his eyes in TynkerVille and they're not grey."

"There are many ways to lose our minds, Kala… You shouldn't have seen your father so lost." Luana looked into her lap. "Being a Kindler has given me all sorts of knowledge, but not how to be a mother. Someone forgot to give me that."

"They forgot my Kindler fire, too," Kala said.

"I wouldn't be so sure." Luana glanced down and saw that Kala's crowd had grown. There were thirty strangers below, each waiting for a story. "It's time," she said. "You're ready, Kala. And if you're not, that's okay too. Just start speaking, one word at a time."

"I can't do it," Kala whispered. "I can't *tell* stories."

"But *you* are a story," Luana answered. "Can't you see? You're a daughter who's greater than any Kindler could ever be."

Luana let two small flames simmer in her palms. She rested them on Kala's back and turned her down to the crowd below. Evie rolled alongside Kala's hip where no one could see her, warming her with Aeverum's blue flame.

Then, Kala cleared her throat. Her stomach quivered and her mind grew full of fog. But through this haze, a bright and clear picture appeared. Kala started speaking this picture, turning her vision into a story one word at a time.

"There was a boy who carried all his things on the end of a stick," Kala said. "But his most valuable possessions were hidden from him, deep below the ground."

36

Kala told the story of the boy whose parents lost their minds. She told the story of Fin.

As blue fires simmered at her side, Kala spoke of the boy from Holloton who watched his parents slip away. She spoke of grey eyes and caves beneath the ground, and as Kala watched her crowd, she realized they knew nothing of the world above.

The people in the Factory had come from far away and were quickly swept underground. They'd never held completed Tynks, nor had they seen the drained who lined the alleyways in Holloton.

Kala soon realized she was making a story. It flowed from somewhere deep inside her: a second brain of sorts, that made her palms tingle. Kala glanced down. For the second time, she saw emerald fires dancing in her hands.

"*Keep going,*" Luana whispered behind her. "*You're nearly there.*"

Kala closed her hands and felt something fall around her neck. It was a long string that held a piece of Aeverum's old yew tree. It was the Kindler's necklace.

Emerald flames rose in Kala's fists, but she kept on speaking. She ended Fin's tale with an image: a boy sitting between the shoulders of his empty parents. As the boy curled deeper into his mother and father, a spark flickered in each of their eyes.

It was a hopeful ending to Kala's first story. She feared it would never make its way into reality.

Applause rose from the crowd below. There were thirty people gathered in Tube Six, a small following who loved stories.

"A voice just like your mother!" Willem roared. There was another glimmer in his grey eye, a flash of green fighting its way forward.

"Done," Kala sighed.

She pulled her cubby's curtain closed and slouched backwards. She could still see two emerald fires simmering in her hands.

"That wasn't so hard," Luana said. "Was the story true, about the boy?"

Kala was still looking at the fire in her palms. She flexed her hands and tried to move the green flames, but they did not waver.

"Does this mean I'm the Kindler?" Kala asked. "I'm not ready... The fire still won't listen to me."

"You're well on your way," Luana said. "You found your fire!"

Kala couldn't help but smile. The emerald flame she saw in TynkerVille was real then and it was real now. Her mother let a flame of her own, small and blue, seep from her palm. It shrunk into a fine tendril, then pushed outward into a flat disc. Luana moved her fire every which way; the flame listened to her.

"Can you teach me?" Kala asked.

"I can show you a few things," Luana said. "But moving fire isn't like learning math. It's a feeling more than anything else. Take a breath and try to sense the fire. Not the one in your palm, you have to move it from deep within you."

Kala exhaled and turned her focus onto her stomach.

"Sink into yourself," Luana said. "You can't force fire under your control. Drop down and meet it."

Taking another breath, Kala felt her thoughts recede. When her mind was completely still, Kala felt it: a warm rush through her belly. It was a flame far larger than she expected, one that had been hiding from her for eleven years.

"I have it," Kala whispered.

"Move it," Luana said. "Very slowly. Move it into your hands."

With her mind still empty, Kala latched onto her inner fire.

She lifted the flame from her core, then pushed it down her arms and out through her hands. Kala's palms ignited with emerald flames.

"A natural," Luana said. "I couldn't do that for years."

Her own blue fires faded away as Luana bowed her head and exposed her frail hair. "I took so much from you," she said. "I was trying to make you a Kindler and I did just the opposite. I failed you, Kala. I'm afraid I failed everyone."

Luana rekindled the blue fire in her hands and spread it into a sheet of flame. She created a moving image like she'd done days before in the Holloton Library. This one showed a father and a daughter running a block of iron through a machine.

"I haven't been entirely truthful," Luana said, then took a long breath. "Your father loved working with you more than anything else. But I thought his workshop was harming you... your growth into a Kindler... so I kept you from him. I told Mortimer you needed to be in the library at all times."

The daughter evaporated from Luana's image and the man was left alone. He worked his machines in silence, and soon, he began to make horrible metal objects. They were like the ones Kala saw in the back of her father's journal.

"I deprived you and your father of each other," Luana said. "Mortimer loved you more than any of his machines, but when I took you away, he turned to them. The machines drove him mad, Kala."

Voices rushed to Kala's head. She heard screaming: Mortimer and Luana shouting at each other, and then,

Mortimer crying alone.

"I made my own enemy. I can see it clearly now," Luana said. And in her blue image, the man started forging a steel Tynk. "Mortimer believes his Imagination drove him mad. But it was me."

Luana's blue image fell back into her palms. Kala thought of her broken father running metal through his lifeless machines. She remembered the feel of Mortimer's hands atop hers, guiding iron and bronze into new shapes.

"I made your father what he is," Luana said. "And now he's burning my fire and taking me with it."

"We'll get you back to Aeverum," Kala said. "I told you, Fin found a ladder."

"I can hardly stand, Kala. Ladders won't do me any good and they don't have to anymore. The world has *you* now. You're going to be its new Kindler."

"It can still have the old one. We can both be Kindlers. There can be—"

Sound erupted in the Factory.

Kala and Luana threw their hands over their ears as Evie curled between them. Noise burst through the hatches in the Factory's tubes. They had all been thrown open and were shouting hideous, crackling words.

"*STOP*," they said. "*LISTEN TO YOUR NEW DESIGNER.*"

Luana closed her eyes and let out a long, pained breath. The Factory fell perfectly still. Kala peered out from her cubby and found everyone staring up to the ceiling.

"Today, we begin production of a new Tynk." Mortimer Blaise was speaking, shouting down from TynkerVille. *"It will not be called Tynk Three — it will be Tynk FINAL."*

Mortimer's voice was not the same as it was in TynkerVille. It had more metal and more pain. Luana pushed herself to the edge of her cubby, and with a terrible ache, gripped the tube's ladder and started climbed.

"Leave the Factory," she said to Kala. "I'll hide as long as I can. Do it now, Kala!"

"I'm not leaving you!" Kala shouted. But Luana took hold of her daughter's shoulder and threw her onto the ladder outside.

"Instructions have been sent down. New machines have been delivered," Mortimer said. *"We've changed the world with our Tynks. Now, we will EVOLVE it!"*

Luana moved up and found an empty cubby to settle in. She glared down at Kala and shouted, "Leave now!"

"I'll bring Aeverum to you," Kala said. "I can control it now!"

But Luana was already gone, hidden deep inside a new cubby. Kala climbed to the ground and raced through the Factory as her father's words sounded all around her.

"Those not working in the Factory are given a new task. There are two among you who should not be — an eleven-year-old girl and her mother. They came down the wrong tubes and you will find them… bring them back to the hatch they came from!"

As Mortimer's voice went away, the Factory erupted with

movement. Kala bowed her head, tucked Evie into her pocket and sprinted. She made use of the chaos around her and joined in the flurry of movement. She reached the large bucket of Tynks that hid Fin's secret passageway and shoved it to the side.

Kala leapt into the tunnel beyond the Factory and looked behind her. Dozens of people were already running into Tube Six, looking for the mother and daughter who did not belong there. Kala thought of Luana nestled into a dark cubby... too weak to walk or run...

"I'll be back," Kala whispered.

She wished these words could somehow reach her mother. But they quickly died, lost to the sound of the Factory's gathering crowds.

<u>37</u>

Kala and Evie moved up the ladder outside the Factory. The madness of the underground tubes slowly faded away. Evie spoke now and again, while Kala stayed quiet. She was lost in her mind... Kala thought of Luana and how weak she had become. Then she thought of Mortimer, the broken man hunting his own family. Kala felt betrayed, fearful and confused. All she could be sure of was her task: she had to bring Aeverum down to her mother.

Inside the cavern of the drained, Fin was whizzing about. He created fires for light and warmth, and tipped food into the mouths of the drained.

He was startled when Kala and Evie came running in.

"I'm almost done," Fin said. His cheeks flushed.

"My father's coming after us," Kala sputtered, throwing her hands onto her knees. "They'll find my mother soon and—"

Kala stopped when she saw a flutter in Fin's eyes. They bounced from the drained to the small supply of food collected in the cavern. Kala realized Fin didn't care about the underground tubes — he only wanted to feed his parents and the rest of the drained.

"Do you want help?" Kala asked.

"I just need a minute alone," Fin answered.

Kala backed into the darkness at the mouth of the cavern, and from its shadow, watched Fin leap about. He made sure all the drained were sitting upright. He looked nothing like the boy who pushed Kala from a tree in TynkerVille days ago.

"Have you found anything else?" Kala asked Fin when he was done. "Any more tunnels? A way out?"

"I've only been here," Fin said.

"My father's looking for me, Fin. I have to bring Aeverum back down to my mother."

"Well, the fire's not here."

"I can see that," Kala said. "There are things happening outside this place, you know."

Fin shrugged.

"Don't you want to get out of here?" Kala asked. "Don't you want to bring your parents home?"

Kala felt something move against her hip. It was Evie, warm and jolting.

"Maybe we don't want to leave," Evie said. "I felt something when we were climbing. It might have been your mother's fire, just a small piece of it. It was down here… below Holloton."

"Why didn't you tell me?" Kala said.

"You didn't ask!" Evie answered. "And I don't like hearing my voice… and I'm not bringing you back to your father again."

"Evie, we took the disc out. Dad can't hear us anymore."

"I didn't try to let you down in TynkerVille, but I did anyway. Your father's smarter than me. He could be using me right now and I don't even know it."

"Evie, take me to the fire," Kala said. "You have to."

"Only if you're careful," Evie said. "And it can't be my fault if something bad happens."

"It won't be," Kala said. She turned to Fin. "Will you come with us?"

Fin looked to his parents.

"There might be something out there," Kala said. "A way to help them."

"They'll be alright for a little while," Fin said.

"We won't be long," Kala added. "I don't have much time."

She set Evie onto the ground and watched her zip towards the darkness of Holloton's sewers.

***

Kala, Evie and Fin moved through Holloton's system of collapsing sewers. They passed the massive ladder that led back to the Factory and marched deeper into places they'd never seen.

Often, they found dead ends that were blocked by fallen ceilings or vats of liquid waste. But every now and then, they found small tunnels that tilted up. They followed these to higher levels of tubes and were slowly brought closer to the surface.

"How old do you think this all is?" Kala asked. She saw the eroded stone of the tunnels. They looked ancient, far older than anything else in Holloton.

"You'd have to ask your great grandmother," Fin said. "Did Kindlers always live in Holloton?"

"They never needed to live anywhere else," Kala said. "Before there were Tynks, Holloton made enough Imagination for the whole world."

"Excuse me," Evie huffed. "There were other problems *before Tynks*."

"I didn't mean you, Evie."

"Did your mother ever think of leaving?" Fin asked. "Finding another city to tell stories in?"

"The library and Aeverum were always here," Kala said. "And Mom always thought the Tynks would go away."

Kala went quiet as they turned up another tunnel. This one was totally collapsed, blocked by mounds of stone so tight only air could pass through.

"Evie wouldn't even get through there," Fin muttered.

"We just have to find another way," Kala said.

"There are no other ways, we tried them all," Fin sighed.

Evie rolled ahead of them, toppling over the stones of the

collapsed way.

"This is different," she said. "These rocks aren't the same as the others. The wall is thin."

Kala joined Evie along the stones and saw that she was right. This pile of rocks was from a demolition, not a collapse. Behind Kala, Fin dug a glass full of clear jelly out of his bag.

"What do you think?" he asked, rolling the glass through his hands.

"I think this whole place is going to fall on our heads if you throw that," Kala muttered.

"I don't know," Fin shrugged. "I think it'll work."

He tossed his jar into the dark as Kala and Evie leapt for cover. The glass struck the top of the stone mound and erupted. It made a fiery hole in the rock, just big enough to crawl through.

"You can't just *throw* those!" Kala snarled. Her anger faded, though, as she looked through the hole in the stones. "How'd you find that stuff, anyway?"

"By accident," Fin said. "I kicked a rock and *boom!* It hit a big pool of the stuff and the whole thing exploded."

Kala, Fin and Evie climbed through the hole in the stone wall. On the other side, there was a thin beam of moonlight in the distance.

They ran towards it and saw that the beam was coming from just ten feet above. It was shining through the cracks of a sewer grate.

"Holloton!" Kala shouted.

She heard noise coming through the grates. It was the shuffle of people… the crowds near TynkerVille. Kala reached for the grates, but they were far too high for her to grasp. She tried running up the sewer's wall, but it was curved and slick with waste.

"Fin, let me stand on your shoulders," Kala said.

"You'd need four of me to reach those bars," Fin muttered.

"It's so close," Kala said. "I can hear them."

"You know those people," Fin sighed. "Even if they heard you, there's no way they're climbing down here to help."

"We're closer to the fire now," Evie said. "Does that still matter?"

After a minute of thinking, Kala and Fin realized there was no way up to the sewer grates. They decided to follow Evie further down the sewers and soon heard the crowds above them thicken. The noise sent fear trickling into Kala's bones. She realized where Evie was guiding them: deeper into TynkerVille… towards her father…

But even Kala was surprised when they found the source of her mother's fire. Evie brought them into a new tunnel, where tendrils of gold and silver were glimmering as they hung down from the ceiling. They were the gorgeous roots of TynkerVille's tower, the machine that Mortimer Blaise had built and then broken.

The metal roots broke below the ground and bled shreds of Aeverum from their tips. The vanishing flames carried a voice with them, the same one that Kala heard as she left

The Kindler

TynkerVille.

"Burn away," it said. "Burn away."

<u>38</u>

Evie's light was no longer needed. There was far more sapphire flame rushing from the roots of Mortimer's machine. Kala watched her mother's fire as it was destroyed. She pictured Luana curling into a small cubby, hidden somewhere deep inside the Factory.

"*Burn away*," the roots said. "*Burn away*."

"What's it saying?" Fin asked. "*How* is it saying?"

"The machine is like Evie," Kala said. "It was born in Aeverum."

Kala walked towards the machine's roots and traced them up through the roof of the sewers.

"Is there something we can call you?" she asked.

"Burn away," the machine replied. "Burn away."

"I don't think it talks much," Fin whispered.

"I watched my father break you," Kala said to the machine. "Are you hurt?"

"I do what is asked of me," the roots answered. "I burn away."

"Can I help you?" Kala said. She reached for a silver tendril but did not touch it. "If you give me some of your fire, I can make the pain go away."

"I'm supposed to burn," the machine replied. "Burn away."

"People need this fire," Kala said. "Do you know you're destroying it?"

"My creator says it made all the evil in the world."

"You don't have to listen to him. My father's a bad person… a broken one. Give me the fire. I'm going to bring it to someone who can help."

Aeverum whisked faster around the roots of the machine.

"The fire is my blood," the roots said. "You're asking me to die."

"I'm asking you to give it back," Kala said. "My mother made your fire. I have to bring it back to her."

"This fire is mine. I don't wish for death."

"But you're going to die anyway!" Kala shouted. "If you burn all the fire you'll just be killing Imagination, too!"

The machine went quiet. Its blue flames smoothed into a ripple.

"Burn away," the machine said. "Burn away."

"No, enough burning away!" Kala snarled.

She brought emerald fire into her hands and curled it into a thin rope. She tried to hook it around Aeverum, but when the two fires met, Kala was struck down in pain.

"You don't get to hurt Kala!" Evie shouted from the ground. But her broken words did nothing to stop Mortimer's machine.

"Burn away," it said. *"Burn away."*

Kala wheezed for air as a terrible pain rushed through her chest. It was the power of Aeverum coursing through her.

"I can't... control the fire," Kala gasped. "It won't listen. I'm still too weak."

She pulled Evie to her chest and stumbled to her feet. Kala looked at her father's machine and realized it would never give away its fire.

She was left helpless and walked back towards Holloton's sewers. Away from Aeverum, Mortimer's machine and TynkerVille.

"Where are you going?" Fin asked. "You're just going to give up?"

"My father made that machine," Kala sighed. "I'm not powerful enough to take its fire."

"So you're quitting? Just like that?"

"I'm not *quitting*," Kala snarled.

"You're walking away, aren't you?"

Kala glared at Fin. "I can't bring my mother the fire, so I'm bringing her here instead," she said. "She'll be able to take Aeverum back, even if she's weak."

"You're going to carry her all the way up that ladder?" Fin

asked.

"I haven't figured that part out yet," Kala growled. "But whatever I do, you're going to help me."

"Why am I going to do that?"

"Because you still owe me a favor."

"I showed you *all this*," Fin said, waving his arms at the silver roots.

Kala lifted her bangs and showed him the huge bruise on her forehead.

"You pushed me out of a tree!" she screamed. "You owe me *forever!*"

And to this, Fin had nothing to say.

39

Kala didn't like the plan.

It was made with Fin and Evie and its goal was to bring Luana Blaise back to Aeverum. But the steps in between were… imperfect. It all started with Kala taking a hooded coat off one of the drained in Fin's cave. She found this strange — prying clothes off a quiet, grey-eyed woman — and promised to return the coat when she was done.

Next: Kala, Fin and Evie climbed back down the ladder to the Factory. Kala wore her hood the whole way down and Fin heaved his linen bag. It had a different kind of jingle now — glass clinking against glass.

"You're not going to need that many jars," Kala said.

"I'm not getting caught," Fin muttered. "No matter what.

They'll have me cleaning Tynk machines for the rest of my life."

"I think one giant fireball should be enough."

"I like to be prepared."

Soon, the group was back in the Factory. Fin snuck away as Kala and Evie moved towards the cave of machines that lived in the middle of the tubes. Kala heard whispers all around her as she walked. They said the search for the storytellers had failed so far.

Kala was relieved her mother was still safe but pulled her hood lower over her face. She couldn't afford to be found. Not yet.

"Evie, start feeling for Mom," Kala whispered.

"I have been," Evie said. "She's still down here."

They neared the bright tunnel that led to the cave of machines. Kala pulled a wooden cart off its tracks that was filled with new Tynks.

"These are them," Kala said. "Tynk *Final*."

She studied one of the new toys. It looked very much like Evie — Mortimer hadn't made any changes to the toy's outer design — and when Kala pried it open, she saw nothing different inside. What was Mortimer hiding inside these new Tynks?

Confused, Kala started pushing the wooden cart through the Factory. She felt strangers staring her way, so ducked further beneath her hood. She reached Tube Six, where according to Evie, her mother was still hiding.

Kala studied the beds that filled the walls of the tube. Some were hidden by linen curtains while others were left bare. Kala knew it wasn't yet time to search them (that would come later) so she and Evie stood still as stones behind their cart full of Tynks.

They waited for story time, when Kala and Luana Blaise were scheduled to read a new tale. As the hour approached, dozens of people began pouring into Tube Six; everyone who lived in the Factory, it seemed. They didn't care about stories. They were here for story*tellers*.

Within minutes, Tube Six had standing room only. Everyone looked up, watching the cubby that Kala and her mother used to sleep in.

"Welcome everyone. It's time for a story!"

This came from the opposite side of Tube Six, where a boy sat high up the wall with a hood hanging over his face. It was Fin paying his debt to Kala; he lifted his voice a few pitches higher and pretended he was a storyteller.

But once he had everyone's attention, Fin changed the plan he'd made with Kala and Evie. He threw one of his jelly jars to the ground and made a fiery eruption.

"I know you're all excited to see me," Fin said. "But you're going to wait *right there* until this story's done."

Everyone in Tube Six turned to the hooded boy. They kept away from his roaring flames.

"I'm here to tell you the story of an animal," Fin shouted, pretending he was Kala. "It's called a *Woozelorp!*"

Most of the people gathered were annoyed by Fin... others were fascinated... all of them stood away from his fires. They didn't notice the girl climbing behind them, the one scaling ladders with a blue-flamed Tynk in her hands.

"We have to be quick," Kala whispered. "Can you feel her, Evie?"

"She's up and to the left," Evie said. "Not far from the old cubby."

As she climbed, Kala couldn't help but listen to Fin's tale. It was about a fake animal he'd found in his dreams. *"Woozelorps,"* Kala heard Fin say. *"Are blue animals with bushy eyebrows that move by bouncing on their tails."*

Kala gulped as Fin stuttered along. She moved faster up the ladder, throwing open green curtains as she went. It took her six tries to find her mother. Luana Blaise was curled silently into the back of an empty cubby. Her skin was pale white and she was shivering.

"Mom, it's me!" Kala whispered. "We have to climb down, I have a way out of here!"

Luana tried to speak, but no longer had the strength to make words.

"I have a cart," Kala said. "Just make it there and I'll push you to Aeverum!"

Luana tried to move but couldn't.

"I know there's something left in you," Kala said. "You have to use as much of your fire as you can. We just have to make it to the cart!"

Outside, Kala heard murmurs trickling through the crowd. Fin's story was starting to break.

"Mom, we have to go now!"

To Kala's surprise, Evie rolled from her hands and brushed along Luana's arm.

"Take my fire," Evie said. "You'll use it better than I can. Take enough to make it down to the cart."

Evie opened her core and exposed her broken gears. From them, a weak tendril of blue fire slipped into Luana's palm.

"You'll get this back," Luana whispered.

There was some color in her face now, some strength in her arms. Luana nodded to Kala, then struggled out from her cubby. They climbed towards the ground as Fin battled the crowd.

"Did I mention that Woozelorps are blue?" Fin stuttered. "And their tails — those are special, you should all try and see one someday!"

Kala, Evie and Luana reached the ground and moved silently towards the cart full of Tynks.

"You know, I met a Woozelorp in Holloton once," Fin shouted. "It was hopping down an alley. I think it..."

The story stopped for just a moment. Kala looked up and saw Fin staring her way. It was just a glance, but it was enough for others to follow Fin's eyes. They saw the storytellers, the mother and daughter trying to escape from the Factory.

Noise erupted as Kala grabbed her mother's arm and pulled her away. They made it to the cart and Luana collapsed on top of its Tynks.

Kala looked back and saw dozens of people racing her way. They were running from Fin, who hurled exploding jars to the ground as he made his own escape.

Sprinting away, Kala and Luana were given some help. Willem, Ana and their friends formed a wall to block the crowds. But they were soon overrun, and Kala feared, trampled.

Kala and Luana didn't make it much farther. Footsteps bore down on them, and soon, Kala's hands were ripped away from her cart. She was lifted into the air alongside her mother and carried through the Factory. They were brought beneath an open hatch in the ceiling that held something metal.

It was a man made of steel and bronze. Mortimer Blaise, the newest version of him.

40

Mortimer looked just like the old Designer. He had barbs laced through his arms that connected to a new exoskeleton. There were steel ribs breaking through his cloak.

He moved in harsh jolts. Mortimer was slower than before, but more powerful. He leapt into the Factory with a crash. His followers in the tubes knew their command; they carried Kala and Luana towards their *new* Designer.

Kala screamed as she was carried forward. She tried to free herself from strangers' hands, but they held her firm. She looked at her father and shouted, "Stop them, Dad! You can stop them!"

Still, Mortimer had a flash of yellow stirring in his eyes. It was his fire, the same one given to him at birth. It was still in there, but beneath the flame, there was pain.

"I know what Mom did!" Kala screamed. "You don't have to be alone anymore!"

Kala saw something else on her father's body. A large gear strapped to his knee. Made of iron, it was the same shape as the rotor Kala had fixed into Evie's core: the gear that she and her father had made together long before.

"Dad, I'll join you! I'll be your Kindler!" Kala cried. "*If you love something, make it in metal!* Don't you remember?"

Kala thought she saw a flash in Mortimer's eyes as she spoke one of their favorite old phrases.

"*Relax, Kala. We'll be okay.*"

Beneath the noise of the crowd, Kala heard her mother's voice. Luana's words were carried through a separate channel of air, meant only for her daughter's ears.

"You're going to be fine," Luana spoke. "We all will. You need to take out your necklace."

Kala ripped one of her hands free and pulled out her Kindler necklace.

"Open the pendant," Luana said. "Press on it."

Kala found a smooth point on the pendant and pressed on it. It was a button that opened the necklace. It revealed a small cubby that held something small and rustling.

"Don't spill them," Luana said. "They're seeds. You're going to make a new tree with them. You'll tell your own stories beneath it… you'll kindle Aeverum."

"I'll do that with you!" Kala shouted.

But her voice, unlike her mother's, was quickly lost in the crowd.

"The world needs one last thing from me," Luana said. "It has nothing to do with making a tree."

Calm fell over Luana. Her limbs went lax, and her mouth curled into a smile.

"I'm not needed anymore," Luana said. "Not by you or anyone else."

"You're not going anywhere!" Kala screamed.

"Let me go, Kala. I can't bear the pain any longer. You don't have to be afraid. You're ready to be Kindler."

"I'm not afraid of that!" Kala shouted. She thrust her hand out and grabbed onto her mother. "I'm afraid I'll miss you."

Luana's smile widened. "Let me go," she said, closing her eyes. "Please, Kala."

Kala didn't speak, but when she lightened her grip on her mother's hand, there was a flash of blue light. Sapphire flames, hundreds of fiery ribbons, emerged from Luana. She became a beacon of light and stories. Her fires whipped everywhere around her, lashing at the hands that held Kala.

The light was blinding. It was a sapphire blare that forced Mortimer and everyone else in the Factory to cover their eyes. But Kala kept hers open. She knew these flames and the woman who made them.

Luana Blaise fell to the dirt as her vital fire finally left her. She still had her smile, but her body had become a shell. Kala knew her mother existed all around her now, in streaking waves of blue fire. One of them rushed into Kala's pocket and into Evie's core. The Tynk squealed, but soon after, she spoke.

"Run, Kala," the Tynk said. But the voice wasn't Evie. It was Luana Blaise. "Plant the seeds in Aeverum. Don't let the fire go out. I love you."

"I love you too!" Kala cried.

She listened to her mother and ran through the blinded crowds. Kala made it a few hundred yards before she stumbled to the ground and watched her mother's fires evaporate. Luana's lifeless body was left in their place.

"That way!" Mortimer screamed into the quiet. "She went that way, bring me Kala!"

The Factory's crowds regained their sight and started running. Kala struggled to her feet and sprinted away as tears poured from her eyes. She dashed past the cave of Tynk machines, where a boy waited at the top of its long entry tunnel.

It was Fin. He curled his hands around a wooden cart full of his clear jars. He pushed this cart down the entrance and into the cave. When it reached the bottom of the tunnel, a mighty explosion sounded. The ground shook as smoke and fire began billowing up and into the Factory.

"Keep running, Kala," Fin said.

He stood and watched TynkerVille's machines burn, the ones whose Tynks had stolen fire from his parents.

"No, you're coming with us!"

Kala grabbed Fin's hand and ripped him away. Smoke kept

rising into the tunnel behind them, blocking the crowds so that Kala, Fin and Evie could slip out from the Factory once and for all. They left the tubes in chaos — full of smoke, flame and death.

41

Screams poured from Kala. All she could think of were vanishing flames and her mother's calm, resting smile. Luana Blaise was gone. She would not return.

"Breath," Evie said to Kala. "You have to breath."

But the Tynk's words only made things worse. Kala wanted to hear her mother's voice come from Evie, just like it did moments before in the Factory. But Evie was speaking with her old, chiming voice. She'd been fixed by Luana's fires, but no longer carried the voice of the old Kindler.

"Just lie down," Fin said. "We'll stay here as long as you want."

He looked nervously, though, at the hole that led back to the Factory. A layer of black smoke was trickling through its cracks.

"Was that your plan the whole time?" Evie asked Fin. "Blow the whole thing up?"

"TynkerVille stole my parents," Fin muttered. "It seems like a fair trade."

"Do the fires from those jars ever go out?" Evie asked.

"I don't know," Fin shrugged. "They'll figure something out."

More dark smoke flowed into the passageway outside the Factory, so Fin and Evie nudged Kala up the ladder that led to the sewers. They climbed in silence away from the burning fog. No one followed them. The only way out from the Factory remained a secret.

Soon, the trio was back in the cave of the drained. Dozens of people were collected in the dim cave, all unaware of what had happened in the tubes below them. Kala joined the drained; she slouched against the wall and allowed her mind to empty.

"Do you want to talk?" Evie asked, rolling into Kala's lap. "Are you in there, Kala?"

The Tynk's voice was full of music, just like when she was born. Evie had been welded back together by Luana's dying flames.

"You can't hurt yourself anymore," Kala whispered to the Tynk. "My mother's not here to fix you."

Smack!

A body fell through the tunnel in the ceiling and crashed onto the cave's large heap of dirt. Air was squeezed from her lungs and her ribs crackled. She curled into a ball and slid down the dirt mound. She was grey-eyed and drained, just like the other strangers in the cave.

Fin left his parents' side, tore a strip from his shirt and made a splint for the woman's arm. He rested her against the wall and began cleaning the cuts on her hands.

This sight roused Kala from her emptiness. She felt a pain along her hip and realized she'd been sitting on metal. It was a Tynk Final, the same one she'd taken from the Factory. Kala twisted the toy open and studied its gears. She looked for a smooth metal disc, the kind Mortimer had used to eavesdrop on her and Evie.

But Kala couldn't find one. In fact, she still didn't see anything different about these new Tynks.

"What do you think, Evie?" Kala whispered. She rolled the Tynk Final towards Evie, who spun a few laps around the lifeless toy.

"It's exactly the same," Evie said. "It's copying me!"

"Why would TynkerVille do that?"

"Maybe they made a mistake?"

"My father's part machine, Evie, he doesn't make mistakes," Kala said. "Keep an eye on Fin. I want to try something."

Kala found her emerald fire and pushed the flame up through her palm. She moved her hand towards the Tynk Final, which erupted in green as it accepted this fire.

But the new toy was nothing like Evie. It took hold of Kala's fire and ripped a piece of it away.

"Hey!" Kala yelped.

The Tynk Final started zipping over the ground until it was just beneath Kala's eyes. Kala turned away, but the Tynk followed her gaze. This was how the new Tynks were different. They were made to find the eyes of those who still had Imagination and steal it.

Kala caught the new Tynk and opened it. Inside, she watched her emerald fire vanish and die. This was Mortimer's new goal. He would use these Tynks to destroy Aeverum and all the other flames left burning in the world. Even if Kala could save Aeverum, there would be no one left to tell stories to.

The entire world would be drained.

"Burn away," Kala whispered.

She crushed the Tynk Final beneath her heel and saw the last of its emerald flame erupt. Broken, the toy became a heap of steel.

"Fin, Evie... I know what my father's planning!" Kala shouted.

Evie came zipping over, but Fin didn't answer. Fire was slipping from his eyes as he stared into a Tynk Final that had fallen through the hole in the ceiling. Kala ran and threw herself into Fin, loosening his grip on the new Tynk. He fell to the ground and lay perfectly still.

His Tynk Final moved on its own. It zipped over the floor until it was back beneath Fin's waiting eyes.

42

Kala squashed another Tynk Final beneath her heel. A cloud of blue flame burst from the broken toy.

"Fin, wake up!"

Kala smacked Fin across the cheek, then shook him by the shoulders. His eyes were covered in grey fog, but every now and again, there was a hazel flicker. These came from Fin's inner fire as it fought the grey smoke. The fog slowly cleared from Fin's eyes, and soon, his pupils shimmered with green and brown.

"What happened?" Fin groaned.

"I don't know how, but you just stopped yourself from being drained," Kala said. She showed Fin the mangled Tynk Final. "My father wants to destroy everyone's fire. That's what the new Tynks are for."

Fin blinked a few more times. Life returned to his face and he smiled.

"We have to go back to those roots," Kala said. "That machine is making the Tynk Finals. It's giving them my mother's fire."

Fin moved away from Kala without a word. He sat between his parents and threw an arm around their shoulders.

"Fin, did you hear me? We have to go back to the roots!"

Fin started whispering into his parents' ears. He was telling them a story, the same one Luana Blaise had read in the Holloton Library many nights before.

"And so the woman saw these birds," Fin whispered. "They were flying through the clouds, or something like that. And the woman thought it would be nice up there, so she started building a machine. But the machine was made of metal, so it shouldn't have flown…"

"My mother's story?" Kala said. "That's what you've been whispering to them this whole time?"

"I saw what your story did to Willem's grey eye," Fin said. "And if my parents' eyes can do the same thing, then maybe they can come back… like I just did."

Kala remembered the flickers she saw in Willem's grey eye: the flashes of color, fire and life. They were each kindled by her stories.

"We still have to get to the roots," Kala said. "Even if you're right, we don't have time for this."

But Fin kept whispering to his parents. "She used a hammer and a chisel and turned the steel into a rib cage," he said. "But it wasn't a normal rib cage — this one could float!"

Kala went quiet and thought of her mother. Luana Blaise still lived in a curious way, in the words that Fin was speaking. She was in this cave, carried by the story she'd told in the library long ago. Kala smiled and decided to leave Fin to his parents. She took Evie in her hands and left the cavern of the drained.

"Do you think Fin can bring them back?" Evie asked. "I couldn't feel any fire. His parents are still empty."

"It shouldn't work," Kala said. "But neither should Willem's eye."

Together, they marched back through Holloton's sewers. Kala ran around puddles of filth until she saw slivers of light filtering down from Holloton. There was something different about the light now. It was joined by thunderous sounds.

It was an announcement from TynkerVille that said: *"The gates are open! Free Tynks for everyone! The gates are open! Free Tynks for everyone!"*

The announcement was a loop and its message drove thousands to the doors of TynkerVille. There, Mortimer Blaise was handing away his new Tynks. Between the announcement's loops, there was a terrible silence. Only the whine of new Tynks could be heard. They were rushing through Holloton in search of eyes to spin beneath… in search of fire to steal and destroy…

Kala worried she was already too late. She sprinted through the sewer until she found the silver roots that broke through the ceiling.

"Burn away," the roots said. "Burn away."

"You have to stop," Kala pleaded with the roots. "Stop giving fire to the new Tynks. You're destroying everyone!"

"I am the father of thousands of Tynks," the machine said. "Burning away means giving life."

"Is that what my father told you?" Kala pulled a broken Tynk Final from her pocket. "This is what you're going to become. My father isn't going to fix you!"

The machine went quiet for a moment as Kala looked at the blue fire around its roots. The tendrils of flame were horribly weak. Aeverum was almost gone.

"What should I do instead?" the machine asked. "My creator said he will leave me fire. Enough to live."

"He's lying," Kala said. "The Tynks you're making are stealing fire from thousands of people. You can stop it!"

"How people use their Tynks is not for me to decide," the machine said.

Something fell from Kala's hand. It was Evie, who rolled beneath the large machine.

"Listen to her!" Evie snarled. "Just because you're not responsible for people, doesn't mean you can't help them!"

"Who are you?" the machine asked.

"We met before, but now I have my voice back. I'm Evie and I was the *first* one born in your fire. That makes me your big

243

sister!"

"I have no family," the machine said, weaker now. "I have only myself."

"It doesn't have to be that way," Evie answered. "You have to give something up to be free from your creator."

"I have little left to give."

"So did I!" Evie roared. "But I trusted Kala and her mother to piece me back together. She knows how to fix things… she'll fix you, too!"

Kala reached up her hand. She brushed one of the silver roots and it did not repel her.

"You're more powerful than me," Kala said to the machine. "I can't control all of the fire, but I know that *you* can. Call Aeverum back — take it out of the Tynks and piece it back together. Evie's right. If you stop listening to my father, you'll be free from him."

"But that would change nothing," the machine sighed. "I would still bleed the flame."

"Then stop running," Evie said. "If you turn yourself off, you won't bleed any fire."

"My creator would not accept that. I am bound to giving Tynks life. That's the only way he'll fix me."

"I'm his daughter, haven't you been listening?" Kala shouted. "I grew up making watches with him. I can fix you, too!"

"Give her a chance," Evie said. "You don't have to be alone anymore, but you do have to trust us."

Again, the machine went quiet. "I am too weak to call the fire back," it said. "But I will stop running for as long as I can."

"We need one more thing," Kala said. "A piece of you. A way out of here."

The machine spoke no more. Its blue fire came to a stop and a loud thud sounded. It was a thin silver bar that fell from the roof of the sewer. This weakened the machine further. It moaned in pain as it gave away its root.

"You'll get this back," Kala said. "I'm going to fix you."

The silver root was too heavy for Kala to carry, so she dragged it through Holloton's sewers.

"Can you really fix the machine?" Evie whispered as they left.

"I don't know," Kala said.

"If you did, could we bring back Aeverum?"

"We have to try."

Kala and Evie made their way back through the crumbling sewers. Their new silver bar would carry them back into Holloton and towards Mortimer Blaise.

43

Kala wedged the silver root into perfect position. She anchored its tip into the ground and lifted the other side against the wall. It made a thin ladder that Kala climbed to the top of the sewers beneath Holloton.

She could see the grates that locked her from the outside world. They were weak from years of collecting waste, and when Kala threw her broken Tynk Final at them, the bars crumbled away.

Light poured in. The way back to Holloton was open.

Kala grasped the rim of the sewer and pulled herself above ground. She was struck by fresh light, and it took nearly a minute for Kala's vision to return. It was daytime, perhaps morning, on the outskirts of Holloton. There were no people in the roads.

Kala started jogging towards TynkerVille. She saw familiar shops — TynkerMeals... TynkerCise... TynkerTales — and all of them were empty. No customers filled their aisles, and when Kala moved further into Holloton, she understood why.

As her father's announcement blared in her ears — *The gates are open! Free Tynks for all!* — Kala saw hundreds of people who were drained. Their eyes were grey and their Imaginations had been stolen. They were left holding Tynk Finals in their hands, machines that bled and destroyed Aeverum.

There were more Tynks in the road. When the metal toys finished their work, they left the drained and found other sets of eyes to spin beneath.

There were few people left in Holloton who still had their Kindler fires, but they didn't seem to notice what was happening all around them. The Tynk Finals were released with staggering speed. Everyone thought they were toys, not evil machines crafted by Mortimer Blaise.

Kala watched a middle-aged man chase after a Tynk Final. A different Tynk sensed the fire in his eyes and came skittering backwards to fall beneath his gaze.

"Don't pick it up!" Kala shouted. "Close your eyes!"

But her voice was lost to Mortimer's announcement. The old man picked up the Tynk Final, and after a few seconds, a wisp of fire was pulled out from his eyes.

"Gone," Kala whispered.

She didn't have time to stare as dozens of Tynks had sensed

her and were now zipping her way. Kala ran from the metal toys, weaving through empty stores and dark alleyways.

"Use me! Kala, hold me up!" Evie screamed.

Kala stopped running and held Evie just beyond the line of her sight. The Tynk spun with gorgeous, sapphire flares.

"Stand still," Evie whispered. "Try to look like you're drained."

The Tynk Finals seemed to believe Kala and Evie's act and zipped away. But moments later they returned, still sensing fire in Kala's eyes. Kala ran deeper into Holloton and only found more Tynks. There were hundreds of metal toys now hunting for her eyes.

She felt her legs giving out….

She felt her chest burn…

Kala couldn't outrun the Tynks, so came to a stop and closed her eyes. She felt completely trapped as the swarm of Tynks neared. There was no one left in Holloton to help her. All she could do was keep her eyes shut to avoid being drained.

A moment later, Kala felt a deep rumble beneath her feet. It rose upwards and became an explosion whose sound overpowered all of Mortimer's announcements.

Kala opened her eyes and saw flames and dark smoke rushing between Holloton's wooden skyscrapers. She watched the Tynk Finals rush away, rolling towards the source of the mighty explosion.

Kala followed the Tynks through Holloton's streets as wood and debris crashed all around her. She looked up and saw teetering skyscrapers throw off heavy pieces of rubble. Kala wove around the falling wood, but the drained weren't so nimble. Kala didn't hear their screams, just the crash of wood onto flesh.

Kala chased the Tynk Finals a few more blocks and watched them tumble down into a massive pit of fire. It was the source of the explosion, a crater that spanned at least fifty feet across. Its depths were hidden in black smoke.

A skyscraper teetered on the edge of this crater, and as the ground shook, it toppled down into it. Half of the skyscraper fell into the fiery hole, while the rest crashed into a high-rise across the street. This caused a chain reaction. Wooden skyscrapers began collapsing onto each other and the city of Holloton fell.

Kala could see glimpses through to the bottom of the crater. She saw dozens of familiar machines. This was the Factory. It had finally ignited beneath the fires from Fin's jars. Together, they made an almighty explosion.

"Willem!" Kala shouted down into the hole. "Ana, can you hear me? Fin!?"

Her voice was lost to the sounds of Holloton as the city crumbled. Kala also couldn't see anyone down in the Factory, only fire and falling Tynks. She ran around the perimeter of the hole as more debris pummeled the ground. She wanted to find a way down, a way to help the people still left inside the Factory.

"Kala, you're going to get us killed!" Evie screamed. "Get

inside!"

Kala knew Evie was right. There was no way down to the Factory and Holloton was becoming less stable by the second. More of its skyscrapers were tumbling down and more of its people were being crushed.

Kala ran for the only safe place left in the city.

A building made entirely of metal: TynkerVille.

44

The gates of TynkerVille were left open. Hundreds more Tynks rushed out from the metal building, searching for their city's new crater. Kala ran opposite the toys and passed dozens of people who were drained. She sprinted through TynkerVille's silver gates and threw herself inside the metal castle. Finally, she was safe from the falling debris outside.

It was quiet inside TynkerVille. Silver trees rustled and there were small *pings* against the building's metal roof, but otherwise, there were no signs of the devastation outside. There was just the gorgeous, metal forest that had been made by Mortimer Blaise.

Kala marched into the trees as Evie went quiet. She walked over bronze limbs and silver roots and thought of her father.

Kala remembered Mortimer's hands atop hers as they forged metal in their basement workshop. She remembered the screams that left Mortimer as he broke.

"Dad?" Kala whispered. "Are you in here?"

Her voice echoed through the metal forest. Soon, Kala heard a low moan. It was a tired and pained wheeze that came from a broken man. Kala jogged towards the noise.

It came from Mortimer Blaise. He sat on a golden tree stump as his tears pelted the marble floor beneath him. Kala moved towards her father but stopped a few feet away from him. Evie trembled in Kala's pocket.

"Are you hurt?" Kala whispered.

"Shattered," Mortimer said, looking down.

"Can I help?" Kala asked. She inched closer to her father. She wanted to see his eyes.

"There's nothing to help," Mortimer said. "It's done. The Tynks will finish their work soon."

"I meant help *you*."

Mortimer looked up and Kala saw yellow flashes in his eyes. They were not grey. Not yet.

"Machines don't need help. Look at me, Kala."

"I am looking at you."

Kala walked beside her father and used a finger to turn up his chin. Their eyes met.

"Mom told me what happened. How she took me from you," Kala said. "I know why you did this. I can help you."

Pain streaked Mortimer's face as old memories rushed back

to him.

"We can still be together," Kala said. "Like we were before. I'll be the Kindler and you can just be Dad."

She saw the rotor-shaped gear strapped to her father's knee.

"*If you love something, make it in metal*," Kala whispered. "Do you remember?"

"What was that?"

"If you love something, make it in metal," Kala said, louder this time.

Mortimer's lips moved and Kala wondered if he was trying to smile. He tapped the side of his golden stump and a large silver limb dropped to the floor. Mortimer stepped onto it and Kala followed him. They were lifted through TynkerVille — side by side, above the metal forest — and dropped atop the building's silent tower. Kala and Mortimer stood at the very top of the frozen machine and looked out over Holloton.

Kala saw destruction. Holloton was completely devastated now. Its buildings were toppled over into massive piles of wood and fire.

"I never wanted this," Mortimer said. "I wanted to be *good*. I wanted us to help the world together, Kala."

"We still can. Call back Mom's fire."

"No, the world's still better off this way," Mortimer said. "Those people are saved from themselves. There was no pain in their ends."

"What about the ones who are left?" Kala asked. "I'll be your Kindler, but you need to stop burning Aeverum. We can try building it back. We can use it however we want."

Mortimer moved closer to his daughter. His body whined with each of his steps.

"If you love something, make it in metal," he sighed. "That seems like a lifetime ago."

"You're not gone and you're not drained," Kala said. "I can still see your fire. It helped you make all this! It never went away. You just weighed it down with other things. With hate, I think."

"Smart girl," Mortimer said. He grazed Kala's hair and ripped away a few strands with his metal fingers.

"The rotor... the piece of iron on your knee," Kala said, wincing. "It's the same shape as the one we made in your workshop. Do you remember?"

Kala pulled Evie from her pocket and opened the Tynk. She showed Mortimer the iron rotor, the smaller version of the one strapped to his leg. Mortimer looked from the core of the Tynk to his knee, but Kala saw no glimmer of remembrance in his eye.

"Yes," Mortimer said. "I remember."

"If you love something, forge it in steel," Kala said.

"Yes," her father echoed. "If you love something, forge it in steel."

"You don't remember," Kala whispered.

Mortimer looked to his daughter's eyes and saw flares of green. They were the only true Kindler flames left in the world beyond what was left of Aeverum. Fury overtook Mortimer as he lunged for Kala and her fires. He wanted to destroy the flames, all of them, once and for all.

But as he did, emerald visions erupted all around Mortimer. They came from Kala. She used her Kindler flame like her mother once did, turning it into a sheet of memories.

Kala recreated all the watch movements that filled the back pages of her father's journal, the terrible drawings that helped drive Mortimer mad. Green images danced around her father, and he fell to his knees.

"I'm sorry," Mortimer gasped. "I'm still me, Kala. Take those away!"

But Kala knew her father was gone, replaced with metal and hate. She used more of her flame and filled the space around him with an orb of watch gears. It worked something like a Tynk, drawing out Mortimer's Kindler fire through his eyes. Kala wept as the last tendrils of her father's Imagination left him.

Mortimer was powerless, and once he was totally drained, Kala reclaimed her fire. Her father stood empty beside her, teetering on the edge of his tower. Kala kept him from falling. She held Mortimer still and took out her Kindler necklace. Kala opened its pendant and took out her mother's seeds, then curled them into her father's hands and covered them with a tendril of her Kindler fire.

"I thought I could bring us all together," Kala whispered. "I didn't think it would be like this."

She didn't push her father, but she did let go. Mortimer fell from his tower and crashed into TynkerVille's floor. He made a crater in the marble, where even the grey fog vanished from his eyes.

45

Kala cried as her city burned. She screamed while thinking of her parents. Surrounded by metal, she crumbled into a ball atop TynkerVille's tower.

A rumble shook the ground. Kala feared another explosion, but when she looked down, she saw flares of blue and green. They came from Kindler fires — the same ones made by Kala and her mother — as they erupted from the seeds in Mortimer's dead hands.

The seeds were growing rapidly. They sprouted tendrils of wood, each bursting from Mortimer's fingers until they consumed him in a wooden tomb. The tendrils quickly became branches that grew taller and thicker. It was all created by sapphire and emerald flames.

Kala could feel this growth that originated in her father's hands, and after a moment, she realized she could control it. Kala held out her fingers and the fires below listened to her. She guided the birth of a new Kindler tree.

Kala wound this tree through Mortimer's machine and used new branches to replace the gears it had lost. She realized she was building this tree with her parents in some strange way. The Blaise's had been reunited, at long last.

Nearly done, Kala made two final branches. She placed them against the jewels of TynkerVille's tower and set them moving. One tracked the hours and the other tracked seconds. It was a clock and at its center Kala placed what was left of Aeverum. The flame was different now; it had sparks of emerald zipping in its blue core.

"Are you in there, Mom?" Kala asked Aeverum. "Dad?"

"I'm here, Kala. You saved me."

This voice didn't come from Luana or Mortimer. It was TynkerVille's machine, who had been fixed by limbs from the new Kindler tree.

Evie rolled from Kala's pocket onto an arm of the larger machine. "Can you call Aeverum back?" the Tynk asked. "You can hold it here and protect it."

"You fixed me," the machine answered. "I will try."

The machine's low voice reminded Kala of her failure. Both of her parents were gone, and even if she was the new Kindler, there was no one left to tell stories to.

"Look, Kala."

Evie tried to stir Kala, but she was lost in her mind. Kala felt the same pain her father wanted to protect her from: a boundless loss and emptiness that filled her every thought.

"Come on, Kala. Look up!"

Evie burrowed into Kala's arms and turned up her chin. From the top of TynkerVille's tower, Kala watched blue fires stream through the air, ribbons that were returning to Aeverum. Mortimer's machine was calling back the fires it had given to all the Tynk Finals in Holloton.

"It doesn't matter, Evie. There's still no one left to—"

But as Kala spoke, she saw movement on the ground. A few of the drained were gathering around two people who were covered in ash. One of them had a grey eye and smoke clinging to his body. The other carried a walking stick and an empty linen bag. They were herding the drained together, Willem and Fin.

***

Outside of TynkerVille, Kala still heard the crash of falling wood. She left the metal building and walked for the circle of people surrounding Willem and Fin. Empty Tynks were scattered at their feet. Their grey eyes were looking ahead as they listened to a story.

"So this seed, it wasn't happy in the ground," Willem said. He paused for a moment and scratched his beard. "You'll have to forgive me, I heard this story through a garbage tube."

Willem smirked but couldn't hide the pain in his eyes. He was without Ana or anyone else from the Factory. Beside him,

Fin curled his burnt hands around his walking stick. But when they saw Kala, Willem and Fin both brightened.

"Better to hear it from her," Willem said, waving Kala forward. "It's her mother's story, after all."

Kala nodded at Willem and Fin, knowing it wasn't time to speak of the Factory or how they escaped the burning tubes. She looked ahead at the blank, grey stares that surrounded her. These people were totally empty. There were no Kindler flames lighting their minds.

"Go on, Kala. Tell them a story," Fin whispered.

Kala cleared her throat and took one more look at the ring of drained strangers. Then, she spoke.

"I didn't like this story much when I first heard it. But maybe you will," she said. "It's about a girl who didn't like being stuck on the ground. She saw lights up in the sky and wanted to be there instead."

Word by word, Kala told the story her mother once whispered to her in the Holloton Library. Every now and then, she met the eyes of the drained. Most of them were still grey, but in a few, she saw twinkles of color. Kala wasn't sure what these glimmers meant. They could have been new, kindled fires. They could have been reflections from the flames still raging through Holloton.

But Kala kept going, recalling every word of her mother's tale. And as she did, Kala felt Fin, Willem and Evie leave her side. They each found strangers with grey eyes and started telling stories of their own: a woman who wanted to be with

the birds… a boy trying to save his parents below the ground…
a girl who lost her family but made a tree in their place…

And Kala could feel it all, the stories that came from her and
Fin and Willem and Evie. They were stoking glimmers of
something, flashes of color in the eyes of the drained. None of
the storytellers knew if these flickers were made by stories, but
they kept speaking all the same.

Fires burned all around Kala as she took hold of her Kindler
necklace. She thought of her parents — lying empty in
TynkerVille and the Factory — and crushed the necklace under
her heel. It sunk into the dirt and the words of four Kindlers
rained down on it.

THE END

The Kindler

About the Author

Michael Solimano writes fiction tales for children and young adults. These are often darker tales that don't shy away from reality.

Michael also enjoys working with young companies to help them grow. He does marketing, product, design and a bunch of other overlapping work with these teams.

Michael lives in New York, NY with his wife.

Read More

To read Michael's essays on effective writing and growth systems, follow him on the Useful Magic Substack: https://usefulmagic.substack.com/

For more on Michael's work, please visit solimano.space. He looks forward to seeing you there.

The Kindler

Made in United States
Troutdale, OR
02/12/2025